Sasha Queen of Darkness

LM Inc.

Sasha Queen of Darkness

A Novel

By Kysia 'Maxx' McLendon

LM Inc.

This book is a work of fiction. Names, characters, places and incidents are products of the author's imagination or are used fictitiously. Any resemblance to actual events or locales or persons, living or dead, is entirely coincidental.

An *Original* Publication of LM Inc.

©2010 LM Inc.

All rights reserved. No parts of this book may be reproduced, stored in a retrieval system or transmitted in any form or by any means without the prior written permission of the publishers, except by a reviewer who may quote brief passages in a review to be printed in a newspaper, magazine or journal.

Edited by Nisha Washington

First printing December 2010
ISBN: 9781456557584
PUBLISHED BY LM INC.
www.LesbianMemoirs.com
        Atlanta
Printed in the U.S.A.

Contents

Chapter One 1

Chapter Two 11

Chapter Three 19

Chapter Four 29

Chapter Five 37

Chapter Six 43

Chapter Seven 49

Chapter Eight 59

Chapter Nine 71

Chapter Ten 83

Chapter Eleven 91

Chapter Twelve 99

Chapter Thirteen 109

Chapter Fourteen 119

Chapter Fifteen 129

Chapter Sixteen 139

Chapter Seventeen 147

Chapter Eighteen 153

Chapter Nineteen 163

Dedication:

For my mother, Patricia Yanders, who believed in me when I didn't believe in myself, and my grandmother, Ola Clark, who keeps me grounded in faith.
The Author

For Terry, who awakened me from my deep slumber with the tempting aroma of her sweet blood.
Sasha

CHAPTER ONE

She hails from centuries long past, has seen civilizations rise and fall and yet her beauty remains true. She is tall, dark, graceful and seductive. Her tantalizing figure invites a touch. Ebony curls, high arching eyebrows and deep set hazel eyes accentuate her full blood red lips.

She is Sasha, the mother of all Vampyres. Bound by death to eternal life; destined to walk the earth feeding on the misstep of mere mortals. Draining life, as the one who took her own, and enjoying the rendering of body. Sucking and draining that which sustains her now. No pretense and without heed. Some she'd made like herself over the years to have as companions, slaves and lovers.

Sexual in nature, Sasha walks the deserted street of Downtown Los Angeles seeking the next that would join her to satisfy her undeniable lust.

2

"I hate this fucking city!" she says aloud to the night. "How I long for the swelter of New Orleans again." The disasters that brought the city to its knees a few years before forced her and a few of the others she'd created to flee their haven.

Now it is within this fast paced city that she dwells. Sasha prefers a less hectic existence but what is one to do? If within her power it would be the nineteenth century again, a time when the kill was less likely to bring in those dreaded detectives and forensic specialist.

In this time, one had to be careful. Humans in their ignorance refused to believe the Vampyre even existed and that is the way she wanted it to remain.

Strolling along under a cold November moon, she listens as her booted heels strike the pavement. Then she smells it--blood! She quickens her pace and turns into a narrow alleyway. Two men accost a wino who lay cowering against a filthy dumpster.

"Well now, what do we have here?" the smaller of the two thugs asks when he sees her. She notes with a grin that he holds a switchblade. The wino whimpers and seeks to dissolve into nothingness.

"I'd rather play with her than this mutt!" the second says. "She's pretty," he continues, licking his rough tongue over thick lips. The two men leave off their play and advances towards her.

"You boys wanna have some fun?" she asks, moving her coat back to reveal tight black form fitting pants and luscious breast pushing against a red lace camisole.

"Oh yeah baby!" mister switchblade laughs, as he comes close, too close, and places the blade near her throat.

"You won't need this honey," she states, her eyes going from hazel to red. Her pulse quickens at the scent *beneath* his filth. The thirst becomes insatiable so that the game she sought to play dies in an instance. Moving faster than humanly possible, she sends the blade flying from his hand and grabs him by the throat. Fear barely registers in his eyes before her fangs are upon his neck.

They slide easily into him and the first taste of blood makes her clit jump, as it always does.

"What the fuck?" the second one whispers as he watches his friend struggle against her. Fear paralyzes him and that proves to be his undoing. He stands, mouth agape, watching the beautiful woman lap up the blood of his buddy, which flows easily into her mouth.

Then suddenly, there's a snapping sound as she breaks his neck. She flings him into a nearby wall and the one yet alive watches the limp figure crumble to the ground.

Sasha uses long fingers to wipe the corners of her mouth. Her pupil's dilate as rosy tears escapes them. She looks over at the whimpering wino. "Flee! This night you are spared, only because I do not wish to be intoxicated with the alcohol which flows through you."

She turns her attention from him and in one fluid motion, is upon the second man. This one she does toy with, as some of her hunger is satisfied for the moment. The fear in his eyes amuses her.

"Pleeease…" he begs. "Dear God help me!"

Sasha chuckles. She notes the wino inching along the wall and stepping over the dead body to leave the ally, his rheumy eyes never leaving her.

"Humans are such contradictory creatures! You seek to kill your brother and in the next instance call out to something that you cannot see to help you escape your own death," she states.

"I'm soooory!" the man whimpers, as her hands tighten upon his throat. He looks into her eyes and seems to relax. The affects of her hypnosis calms him.

"I grow weary of you little *man*. You are weak and no match for me! **I am Sasha, queen of death, destruc-**

tion, turmoil and darkness. How many other women have you preyed upon?" she asks as she shakes the frightened man like a ragdoll. "Never mind, you would only lie," she said as she draws him to her. With her nail, one that grows three times its normal size before him, she pierces his jugular. She watches, fascinated, as the blood spurt out to her.

She draws it to her mouth, gently as a lover might place her lips upon flesh to suck with passion.

Again her pulse quickens, her sex aroused. The feeling of *completion* washes over her as she feeds on human blood for a time that is innumerable. He fights not, but gives in to being drained. His life force weakens, heart slows and with eyes staring into the one he felt sure he would rape, he surrenders to darkness.

Renee Larue leaves *"The Cellar"* LA's newest and hottest nightclub, and heads for her downtown high-rise apartment off Broadway.

"Hundreds of women in this damn club tonight and I still end up sleeping alone!" she mutters. "At least the drinks weren't watered down and that bartender was hot!"

She walks the three blocks home, her five foot five frame moving on spiked heels. She sports a red satin dress that accentuates her shapely form. Although it is chilly, she wears no jacket.

Her shoulders are exposed through spaghetti straps but the alcohol she has consumed makes her blood warm.

Caramel skin, shoulder length hair and long, thick lashes is her trademark. The green of her eyes and long straight nose suggest a mixture of blood. She is beautiful, yet the meekness of her keeps any conceit away. She is quiet and reserved, the main reason she walks home to an empty bed. Many have beheld her and craved her, but her unintentional aloofness has kept her lonely.

The city is asleep at two in the morning, so she is quite surprised when she sees an imposing figure emerge from an ally ahead. Renee stops, her eyes bulging as she realizes that it is a women.

She is striking! Tall, slim and even through her alcohol daze can see, from this distance, that she is absolutely gorgeous. Her black coat is gothic and the echoes of her footsteps are in themselves, spellbinding.

The woman approaches, continuously wiping her mouth. She looks up and spots Renee. Abruptly their eyes meet and suddenly, as if in a dream, she is directly in front of her.

"Hello, what are you doing out here at night alone?" Sasha questions, as she breathes in the beauty of this woman before her.

Renee finds it difficult to speak. There is something in her *eyes* that hold her. She now confirms to herself that she should not have drunk that last French Connection!

"Umm, well," she begins, pulling her eyes away and feeling a little of her sanity return, "I could ask the same question."

Sasha, for the first time in centuries, feels something tug at what use to be her heart. This beautiful, defenseless and obviously inebriated woman makes her smile at the thought of her previous kills of the night. She also picks up snippets of the woman's mind and sees the setting of the nightclub she has previously vacated.

"Oh well," she says lightly, "I just came from *'The Cellar'* and I believe I left my credit card with the *bartender* so I was heading back to see it I could retrieve it."

Renee smiles at the bartender reference and without thinking, wrap her arms around herself, to cover her heaving breast.

"I don't think I saw you tonight, I would remember if I did," she says, suddenly feeling the night's draft.

Sasha, made to know all, suddenly understands that this is the one she has waited her entire life and *unlife* for. She makes note of the juices that have begun to escape the lace panties she so enjoys.

The way her appetite has increased although she has feed well tonight; the quickening of her pulse and the need of her eyes to *change*. Yet for the first time in decades, she resists. She can smell the woman and the desire has her head spinning.

"Well, I like to be in the background, you know, in a corner somewhere, just observing. I saw you at the bar," she lies, picking up more history.

Renee steals another glance at those eyes and falls instantly in love. "Oh well I just came out for a drink or two, so yes, I stayed at the bar most of the night."

Sasha sees into her loneliness. Sees the women she's wanted and those she's loved. Sees pain, confusion, and a childhood devoid of emotional stability. In her inhuman nature, the thought to take this one on a deserted street comes and goes with a flicker.

Renee's chest heaves and she quickly sobers as she recognizes a familiar stirring.

"I could walk back with you, if you want. I'm just heading home and to be honest, there is nothing waiting there for me, not even a pet."

Sasha notes her honesty and pulls the hypnosis of her eyes back. This one she wants whole and honest, a thing she craves.

"No, let me walk you home. This is not a place to be at night, alone."

Renee hesitates, momentarily, trying not to fall apart. "Okay, are you sure?"

The years of loneliness takes her by surprise. "Yes, I'm sure, the card can wait.' she states. With that, she takes Renee's arm and they walk into the night.

CHAPTER TWO

The apartment is warm and inviting. Pictures of the '*UNDERGROUND RAILROAD,*' of which Sasha had assisted, grace the entry walls. One part of history in which she'd admired. The feeling to resist the kill had been overwhelming during those times, but she'd kept her appetite in check.

"Come in, make yourself at home," Renee states, removing her shoes at the door.

'"Shall I take mines off too?" Sasha asked.

"Uh uh… not a requirement, just what I do," she states, moving through the narrow hall.

Sasha watches her move gracefully through her familiar surroundings. Her senses are peaked with the smells surrounding her: body washes, perfumes, nail polishes, not to mention linen softeners, air fresheners and a host of other fragrances someone peculiar about scents would use.

She steps into the living room and feels immediately at ease. The room is done in red hues. Overstuffed sofa and love seat, marble tables, Persian rugs and scores of books on shelves covering entire walls. Then she sees: mirrors everywhere! Sasha hisses, her eyes coming to life. Her body tightens and she denounces herself for not having taken this woman on the street.

Renee enters the room, having changed into a flowing dressing gown.

"Sorry, you probably noticed, but I think I had a bit too much to drink tonight. Can I get you something?"

Sasha moves into the shadows of the hallway as her breathe stops at the site of Renee.

"No thank you. I just wanted to be sure you got home safely," mirrors temporarily forgotten.

Renee sashays towards her. She sees flashes of chances lost, loves that never were, and everything in between. She looks seductively at the first woman she has invited to her home in the three years, since the 'Meagan' episode, and decides she is getting herself laid tonight by this woman who has captured her soul.

"Well I'm here and so are you. What are we gonna do about it?"

Sasha stands still, the mirrors a threat, yet her desire has again peaked. The shadows are a comfort and this mortal she knows now she must make her own.

"Come here to me," she states, allowing the power of her suggestion take over, for she cannot step into this room and risk her non-reflection be seen.

Renee looks into her eyes and becomes helpless. As a puppet she moves to her, no strings attached, yet pulled powerlessly still. Her body moves gracefully as she comes into the arms of this stranger.

Sasha smiles as she takes what may be her finality, into her arms. The kiss is magnificent as she forces to keep her fangs unexposed. Tongues playfully touch, nibbles are exchanged, and the deep longing of a thousand years is conveyed. Hands explore the outline of Renee's figure, new, yet somehow familiar. The smell of her is maddening here in this forbidden place. Was she just not only hours ago leaving her coffin? What is this thing? What hold does she have that would suppress my nature for the kill?

Renee feels something in this kiss. Is it love or destiny? Something tugs at the back of her mind, yet Renee can't stop because this is the kiss she has dreamed of her entire life! Passion, longing, and completion all wrapped into one motion.

Her nipples hardened, seeking to dig deeper into that which satisfies her craving. The room spins as Sasha traces her form; down the curve of her spine, around to the flat of her stomach up to her breast. Nipples are pinched and Renee pulls away with no breathe left in her.

"Hold on baby," she states, firmly holding Sasha at bay, having no idea that with a breath, she could destroy her whole being.

"Whew, that was nice and you have my body doing some things it has never done! I have never felt this and if you want to, I need to experience this laying down."

Sasha struggles against all that she has known and looks down at this perfection. Her innocence and need is overwhelming. The struggle of good and evil is two thousand years old. Yet should she make this decision here? Shall she yet again *'play God?'*

In all of her years of existence she has not felt this which presents itself now. But her heart is racing, her clit jumping and the need for release is too much to excuse.

"Take me to thy bed baby," she states, allowing her ebony hand to be taken. She follows Renee, grateful there are no mirrors along the way, to her bedroom. The view of her from behind is just as ravishing as affront. The gentle sway of her hips, the falling of her hair, the erectness of her back is too much to bear!

The room into which she is lead is simple. Much different than the rest of the apartment that she has been privy to. A large king size bed draped in wine colored bedding, two nightstands both littered with family photos, a large bureau minus a mirror, and thick curtains that would block out any hint of a morning sun. No pictures on the walls, which Sasha thinks odd, but with cum running down her legs, it seems unimportant.

Renee leads her into the room and abruptly stops.

"I just want to say that I don't normally do this."

Sasha feels something break inside her.

All thought of reason flees as she uses again, her insight and sees the flashes of Renee's being: her lonely childhood, teenage solitude, adult triumphs and failures. And she knows that she will make love to her, yet she will not make her feed from destiny's flow.

"I know you don't. Come and taste of me," Sasha says, and leads Renee to the bed which is her very own. She focuses her will and the room shakes. The moon draws into itself; shadows form and covers the only window made in the room.

A look of perplexity crosses Renee's face, and suddenly she is swept up, high above the floor, and into this strange woman's arms. They twirl in winds unseen, lips locked in passion. Her entire being vibrates as something, *something*, is passed into her soul, She feels a slight prick on her lower lip, taste her own blood and opens her looks to stare into eyes, flaming red.

Then music is suddenly playing softly through her apartment, yet she hasn't put anything on to play! It changes from Classical to Jazz to Hip Hop all in what seems to be an instant! And still they levitate. Clothing mysteriously falls to the floor, and they are naked. Sasha's breast clings tightly to her own, the smoothness of her making rational thought impossible.

"Who are you?" Renee whispers between kisses.

"I am everything you need," she answers, as she lays her to the bed.

"Were we…flying?" Renee asks, as she feels the satin of her sheets.

Sasha runs her tongue along the crevice of Renee's neck, licking and tasting all that is. She lowers her naked body down and at the moment their clitoris' meets she understands that this will never happen to her again. She cannot risk giving her a choice. She shall take her, no invitation shall be offered.

This woman will rule the night with her. Give her comfort, hunt with her, and kill with and for her.

"Yes, my love, we flew and there is so much more we shall do. We shall rule the night and all that is therein. Women shall bow to you and men crumble at your feet. You will not know sickness, disease, or infirmity. Death shall not taste your lips…"

Renee moves her hips up to join hers, nipples harder than she ever thought possible. She wants to let go, but then she thinks, "Where is the music coming from?"

As she tries to stop her hands from stroking the satin skin of the one atop of her, the words of Sasha resounds in her ears, "shall not taste death?" She opens her mouth to object and suddenly Sasha's silky tongue is gliding inside of her and all consciousness cease. The wave is pleasurable yet excruciating!

It has been months since she's had and orgasm not of her own making. Now this perfect woman is indeed in her bed on a night when she thought it would not be so.

Sasha tastes the essence of the one she has chosen. Her long tongue slides in and out, the scent driving her wild. She digs her fingernails into Renee's thighs as her own juices flow to the bed beneath her. Madness clinches her for she smells blood and it can't be denied. Slowly her fangs extend.

Every fiber of her being longs to gives this woman a chance, yet she cannot help her animal nature. Lightly she nibbles the tip of her sex, can feel it harden at her stroke. Sasha seeks that which she knows her fangs can safely sink into. So she moves down further still and with a roar, sinks into the soft flesh of Renee's inner thigh.

She tightens and a moan escapes her lips. "Baby, what..." Renee whispers, just as the pain resonates through her body.

Resisting now, stone cold sober, she feels the bite that is deeper that just passion. A scream escapes her lips and pain engulfs her. Just as she blacks out, she feels the warm release of her own orgasm, total and unexpected, gush from her loins and it is then and only then, that she surrenders.

CHAPTER THREE

Renee awakes to the ringing of her phone. She moves slowly, her head pounding, mouth dry, and body aching.

"Hello?"

"Hey girl, how was "The Cellar" last night? Sorry I couldn't make it."

Renee turns her naked body beneath the disarrayed covers.

"Donna, what are you talking about?" she asks, as she tries to open her eyes.

"You called me on your way to the club!" Didn't you go?"

Head spinning, she runs a finger through her hair. "Damn I can't focus!" she thinks.

"I don't… I don't remember."

"Damn you must've had some serious love at the bar! Wait," she lowers her voice to a whisper," girl you got a warm body in your bed?"

"What?"

"Ooh shit! Your pussy feel messed with? Damn! You get laid?"

Suddenly Renee sits upright. The burning of her inner thigh awakens memories of the night before.

"Oh my God," she whispers. "Donna, let me call you back," she states.

"No you don't! Give me all the juicy details. Was it that fine ass stud from last week? Damn I wanted to do her!"

"Donna, I have to go, I'll call you back," she says, hurriedly placing the phone in its cradle.

"Hello," she croaks hoarsely to the still apartment. She listens intently and hears only the dripping of that damn leaky faucet coming from the bathroom.

Five grand a month and she has to contend with this annoying shit! The thought is fleeting.

Again, the burning sensation and she steals a peek under the sheets. Two small puncture wounds, pale around the edges, stare at her and she remembers! She'd had the most intense orgasm of her life, accompanied by a pain foreign to her.

"Her eyes were…red?" she asks aloud.

Renee tenses and pulls herself from bed. Naked, she ventures through every room. Once satisfied that she is alone, she wraps her arms around her suddenly shivering body and feels fright. She sits down on her bed.

"Do not worry sweet one," a familiar voice resonates through her head, ***"I am near."***

The words cause her to jump and her eyes become as large as saucers.

The drapes of her room are, surprisingly open. The Downtown Los Angeles skyline looms before her, beautiful and ominous, even if on this hazy afternoon. "I never open the drapes," she whispers.

"Sasha?" she asks, as she feels her nipples harden. "Where are you?" There is no answer. For what seems like an eternity, she is still. She stares at the door of her bedroom closet, afraid of what may lay therein.

"Get it together girl. She left and you did *not* just hear that. What you're gonna do is get up, get something to drink, and read the morning paper like you always do." Yet she cannot move. The closet door beckons her.

"Sasha, if you are in there and trying to scare me, you have another thing coming because I write some of the best horror stories in the world!" she states.

There is no reply. Only that damn dripping! "This is bullshit!" she says loudly and forces her aching body to stand. She approaches the closet door, and pulls it open.

She screams as the body of a man, throat ripped out and one eye lying upon his cheek falls upon her! She thrashes wildly, heart beating fast enough to cause a stroke. The aroma of death surrounds her as she falls backwards to the floor. The fear is paralyzing, the body heavy, yet, as she faints, the smell doesn't seem so bad anymore.

"Renee, Renee!" Donna James screams at her friend. "Girl, what the fuck are you doing?"

She slowly awakens, as if from a dream. On the kitchen floor she sits, naked and strangely enough, eating a piece of raw steak.

"Uh, what, what's happening?" Renee looks at the meat in horror and raises her eyes to look at her bewildered friend, the only real friend she has in this world.

"Honey, I'm not usually freaked out but this is some crazy shit!" Donna answers. "This some shit for a new book? Because if it is, my ass is getting half of that million! You're scaring me!"

Renee throws the meat to the floor and reaches for the counter; she pulls herself upright as Donna steadies her.

"Donna, what are you doing here?"

"What the fuck you mean? I drove my ass twenty miles 'cause you called talking about a nigga falling out of your closet!"

Renee gasps, as she shakes her head. She tries to move past her friend but Donna stops her with a firm grip.

"Oh no girl, you look like you *really don't know what the fuck is going on!* Listen to me, this closet shit, I'm driving like a bat outta hell and then find you eating some raw ass meat when I get here! And I mean, *eating* the shit! And we're not gonna mention the fact that you stark ass naked! You gonna tell me what the fuck is happening!"

Her friend does her signature 'hip stance' and Renee struggles to keep from laughing.

Then, the voice, again, **"Get rid of her, for she angers me."** The laughter dies in her throat.

Donna watches as her friend of ten years staggers. Renee's eyes seem to cast a film of rosy red. The curling of her lower lip, Donna does not care for. She takes a step back, her mouth slightly agape, and she, the one who has read and listened to the most horrific shit a black woman in her right mind has ever had to, is scared out of her wits!

"Renee? Honey, what's wrong?"

Renee heads for her bedroom. "Girl I'm fine," she states, as her eyes momentarily clear.

"Tell her you were having a bad dream, I don't care what! Just get her to leave…" the voice says.

Renee turns and, in an instance, she is no longer *'she.'*

"Go from this place and let me be," she says in a voice that is not her own.

Donna, a probation officer in one of the toughest regions in the country, steps back. Afraid, she inches her way to the front door.

"Okay my sister, I'm leaving. You don't have to say it twice!"

Renee visibly struggles.

"Wait, I…girl I think I was having a bad dream. Don't go," she states, as the bites on her leg begins to throb again.

She feigns laughter and leans against the wall.

"Listen, I think I had a really bad dream Donna, but I'm cool."

Donna slows her pace, doubt emanating on her face, "whatever you say. Just put some damn clothes on!"

Renee, a 'seventies child,' is not fazed by her own nakedness. Her thoughts are of the weird feelings she is having. "What the fuck is happening to me?" she thinks. Her heart aches for Sasha's presence and touch, a wild sexual desire appears out of nowhere. Yet she is also angry and bewildered, and quite annoyed with Donna.

"Maybe I shouldn't have given your ass a key," she thinks.

They reach the bedroom and as Renee enters, Donna suddenly stops.

"Damn! You did get some! I can smell pussy from here!" She looks across the room and sees the closet door ajar, clothing and fur coats littering the entrance.

"You must've been sleepwalking or some shit."

Renee takes a pair of sweat pants and a t-shirt from the bureau and dresses.

"Let her not enter this space, it is now mines. I do not like her aura; it would be wise to have her leave. Do not tempt me dear heart!"

"Donna, honey, I think I need to be alone. Thank you for coming over! I don't know what I would do without you, but just now I feel the need for some serious sleep."

Donna opens her mouth to object, and feels the hairs on the back of her neck suddenly stiffen. Renee, in all her beauty, has that grin upon her face again. There is something eerie and out of place here.

"Okay, I said I would leave before! You don't have to tell me what went down last night, and I can take a hint!"

She moves away toward the front door, relief on her face. "Oh my God is this some weird shit!" she thinks, and leaves the suddenly cold apartment.

Renee watches Donna leave and strips herself of clothing. She feels constricted and confined. Her body develops a thin layer of sweat, although it is cool in the room. She is aroused and with a blank look on her face, begins to rub herself.

"Sasha, speak to me baby. I want you and can't get my mind together."

"I will come to you in the night my darling, for the night belongs to me. Lay and wait. Disappointment you shall not know. All you need do is just wait…"

"What did you do to me? Something is not right. Why can I hear you and you're not here? And you *bit* me!" Renee screams, her feelings of arousal giving way to anger.

"I will come to you and lay beside you and give you rest. Trust me. Pain shall touch you nevermore. Lay..."

Renee's eyes are suddenly heavy with sleep. She moves to the bed as if in a dream and climbs in under the covers. With a deep sigh, she slumbers.

CHAPTER FOUR

Sasha lays deep within her coffin, in her own penthouse in Long Beach. She is sleep, yet not sleeping, the sun her very enemy. Her mind reaches out to the one she has claimed. Slight regret and disappointment clouds her as she thinks upon the mistake she has made the night before.

"I should not have infected her! What is this thing if I lack control?" she questions.

Then her mind turns to this Donna person, who she can feel, loves Renee dearly. She hisses, hate for this 'friend,' instantly embedded in her heart.

She feels the woman with the touch of God upon her, and touches upon her mind. "Who are you lady? Will thou be a barrier between me and my destiny? I think not! For I will show you who is god and what she is capable of. I will rend the very skin that keeps your veins intact. I will drink the blood of you… better still; I will make you my dog!

I will bring you to this side of death and see if your wails to your God are fruitful.

Renee belongs to me! Me! Sasha Queen of all! And your God is no match for me! For was it not I who influenced Judas, and is that written anywhere in your history? What makes a man weak but the sight of a woman perfected?"

Sasha's wrath is at its peak as she lays and waits for the sun's setting. Since the creation of her being by Lasore himself, the king of all Vampyre, has she not felt the need to strike down and defend that of her own making! This night she shall! "Donna," she whispers into the mind of her, "**I am all**" and you shall feel my wrath! It matters not that she called you, it matters that you are an interference of what is destined to be mine!"

Donna opens the door to her Cadillac, a gift from Renee, and looks up the twenty-four floors to her best friends' window.

"Girl, I am so worried about your ass!"

She enters the car and suddenly her head resonates with a voice of which she is unfamiliar:

"**I am all**" and you shall feel my wrath! It matters not that she called you, it matters that you are an interference of what is destined to be mine!"

A scream escapes her lips, and her keys fall to the floor. The day is bright and full of life. People along the sidewalk, traffic rushing ahead, a wino or two shuffles along as the Los Angeles smog produces a block out of the sun to which all natives are familiar.

Donna has her eyes straight ahead; her hands grip the steering wheel. "What the hell was that?"

Suddenly a flock of ravens plummet into the roof of her car. They descend on the windshield and without thinking, she slams the door shut. They peck at the windows and she screams! And not for the first or last time this day!

Oh shit! What the…?"

A woman, perfect in beauty, melds as one with the ravens and Donna looks on in horror. The activity on the streets freezes. There is no motion as she sits frozen. A wave of desire hits her body as the woman is nude. She stands, legs apart, on top of the hood. Her breasts are gorgeous and inviting.

Donna has not seen a body of such utter perfection in her forty something years.

"DAMN!" she mumbles, and subconsciously reaches for the cross around her neck.

The mirage hisses, and shows teeth long in fang. Her body becomes transparent and is gone, just as suddenly as it has appeared. The motion of the streets continues, and Donna head clears. Her breathing is labored as she proclaims, "Lord, have mercy!"

She cannot move, and the only thing she thinks is to pray. As she calms down, she suddenly wishes, for the first time that she can remember, that Renee had not called her. She reaches for her keys and starts the car.

"I know I'm not a crazy bitch! What the fuck was that? And what's up with my girl? I probably should stay with her, but damn! That just scared the shit out of me."

She eases into traffic, eyes darting to and fro. There are no more birds in sight, and already the memory is fading. Yet she can't shake the feeling of being watched. Even looking into the rearview mirror is a task because she keeps thinking there will be something staring at her from the backseat.

As she makes her way south and back home to Carson, she finds herself fingering the cross draped against her bosom. It gives her comfort as her mind wanders back to the scene she'd found in Renee's apartment.

"Maybe I shouldn't have left her alone," she thinks, as the sun begins to set. "I've known her for years and have never seen her look like that. Maybe the years of writing those spooky ass stories have caught up to her."

Donna feels something in which she cannot describe. A haunting feeling like something bad looming on the horizon. The freeway is clear as she speeds comfortably along. The sun continues to dip on her right and suddenly she prays she makes it home before dark.

It is just before dusk and abnormally, Sasha rises early. Her fury causes her to risk death. The penthouse which overlooks the ocean, is heavily draped, however, the least bit of sunlight can set her afire, literally.

"That which I desire shall not be taken or removed from me!" She picks up an expensive vase and hurls it to the floor. Her long flowing hair trails behind her as she goes on a rampage.

"When I say get rid of a bitch, you get rid of her! How can you withstand my commands?! I will kill her…no; I will make you kill her while her fucking mother watches!" A painting she snatches from the wall and rips apart with her bare hands.

The sun casts its last rays of the day and dips behind the ocean. Sasha, fangs exposed, opens a nearby window and breathes in the night. She inhales the ocean air, her keen scent seeking blood. The Vampyre uses mental telepathy to seek out that which it needs.

Sasha mind fucks a lone jogger on the deserted beach below and, using the strength and speed that comes along with the gift, is at once upon her victim.

Her anger subsides as she feels the life force rush into her. The woman has no time to struggle and it is over in an instant. With blood dripping from her lips, Sasha casts the body out, miles into the ocean. Her hunger satisfied for the moment, she makes the decision to go to Renee first, and give that bitch Donna a few more hours to live.

Birds fly all around her, the sound of them maddening! Renee struggles to get away but her feet are heavy. She runs as fast as she can, yet doesn't appear to be getting far. Ahead she sees Donna beckoning her, blood pouring from wounds covering her body.

She is terrified and wants desperately to reach her friend, to save her. Then Sasha appears and she is suddenly in her arms, soaring towards the heavens. They are flying, the feeling exhilarating! And she wants her, suddenly and completely. She looks into those eyes and cares not what color they are or were, or are supposed to be; only that she wants to drown in them. Lips full of kisses waiting to be taken, and she claims every one. She feels herself ready to explode as Sasha nibbles her ear and whispers, "Be mine forever and I will show you things you have only dreamed of!"

She feels her hand as it runs gently up her thigh and stops to lightly touch her throbbing sex. A moan escapes her lips as she pushes Sasha's hand firmly against herself and with one motion she is cumming and cumming and then there is pain upon her neck! The skin is broken and she is dizzy and she can't breathe. The clouds turn grey and the night is cold and she looks to the heavens and thunder breaks from nowhere.

Sasha sucks and drains as the pain becomes pleasure and then she is sick to the stomach! From somewhere below, Donna is calling her name. It becomes too much as something like a finger invades her wetness. It finds and touches a spot that causes her to give in and then she is falling! Down she tumbles because Sasha is no longer there, and she knows she will die! Down, down, down until…

She hits the floor next to the bed. A scream flies from her lips and tears pour down her face. Her body is tired and she feels alone and thirsty. And there is a hunger in her that she cannot explain. She curls up on the floor, knees drawn to chest and just cries.

"Please help me! What is wrong with me?"

"I am here dear one, and you shall never be hungry, thirsty or in pain again," Sasha says as she walks into the room.

Renee looks up and her heart melts as she reaches out to this woman who, in one night, has made her love her.

"Come to me, be my queen. You need only ask me."

Renee takes her hand and in doing so, walks to her death.

CHAPTER FIVE

Pain vibrates through her body, every nerve screams. Yet, Renee is aroused. The tip of her clitoris has a new heartbeat of its own. Strangely, it seems to also have grown, it is thicker, fuller, more *there*.

Her thighs are sticky with her own juices. Moan after moan escapes her lips as they soar high into the night sky. This time, they are really flying, this is not a dream.

Sasha sinks her fangs deep into Renee's neck. The salty, warm taste of blood drives her senses completely over the edge. This, however, is different. The woman she holds in her arms is like no other she has taken. This one shall neither be food, nor used as a human slave.

No, Renee she has chosen to take as her mate. She shall know love and eternal devotion. The edges of the universe she shall be given.

Renee endures the pain of 'the kisses,' until she feels her life slipping from her. She weakens, her heart slows rapidly and suddenly she is afraid.

"Baby, I am dying…"

Sasha slows her feeding and takes them quickly back to Renee's bed. She lays her down and in the moonlight, Renee sees the maroon smears on Sasha's ebony face. The tips of her teeth drip fresh blood, and she is suddenly appalled. Her mind clears and she knows that she does not want this. Hell, she doesn't really know what *'this'* is!

She only remembers snippets of the past couple of days and the realization horrifies her.

"No, what have I done? What did I let you do to me?" she whispers, as sleep threatens to take her.

"Shhh my love, you must feed and then the ritual shall be complete. We will rule this world together, you and I."

"Have I let the best lay of my life steal my humanity? The most beautiful woman in the world, is not of this world, yet here I lay, as my blood drips from her lips!" she thinks.

Sasha strips off her clothes and stands before Renee, perfect. Her full, round breast with dark areolas that surround erect nipples, causes Renee's arousal to override all thought.

Her slim waist gives way to shapely hips and legs that seem to go on forever. The smooth, hairless sight of the most private part of her is intoxicating.

Sasha takes one long nail and makes a cut along one breast. Her blood runs freely as she straddles Renee.

"Drink of me my love and we shall be together forever," she says as she lowers the wound to Renee's mouth.

'No! Let me die! You have made me lose my mind!" Renee screams as she struggles beneath her. The strength of Sasha stills her as anger, true anger crosses her face.

Suddenly her eyes are hot embers; her fangs extend before Renee's eyes. The beautiful face becomes a monstrosity, growing ancient with her fury.

"You shall never defy me! I will not watch you die a commoner's death!"

Tears stream down Renee's face as she struggles to keep blood from entering her mouth. She shuts her eyes to close out the sight before her.

The thing that is Sasha laughs, the sound shakes the very foundation of the building. In a voice, dusty with years, she says, "You have accepted the invitation my darling. There is no turning back! You shall thank Sasha, the one who truly rules! Drink now of this blood that is not given to humans freely!"

Renee feels her body go limp. The scent of the blood is unnerving, yet death will not come. She looks at the one atop of her and realizes there is no escape. Vengeance is the last thing she thinks, as she closes her mouth around the wound, and drinks.

Donna sits in bed, her heart heavy and spirit disturbed. She has called Renee at least twenty times tonight, and still, no answer.

"Where the fuck is you, I need to tell you about, something…" She frowns as she tries to remember why she needs desperately to get in touch with her best friend. "Something about, birds?" she asks the empty house.

"Oh fuck it! What I really need is to get laid!" Donnas' sex drive is insatiable. She is lonely, but rarely alone. She is a full figured woman, dark in complexion with deep set dimples.

Her style is a bit out dated, but it works for her. Three inch heels to add to her short frame, skintight jeans and halter tops suit her just fine in the California sun.

Her hair she sports short and curly, rarely seen without large gold hoops dangling from her ears. She is saucy and sassy, but her insecurities have led her to much heartache.

"Girl any woman would be lucky to have you!"Renee often says.

"You damn right my sister! Look at all I have to offer," she would answer, hands on her hips.

That never ceased to get Renee rolling with laughter. "Girl your ass needs to quit!"

"Umm what you say? This body here has more cushions for the pushin' and you best believe that shit!"

The two friends would laugh until tears ran down their faces.

Secretly Renee knows of Donnas' insecurities and hopes one day she will believe in herself enough to stop allowing crack heads, maniacs and lowlife's to enter her life. She'd witnessed them come and go over the years, but being as non-judgmental as she is, she could never bring herself to criticize her.

Donna shakes off the feeling she has and picks up the telephone. She begins to dial Renee again but as her eyes cloud over and a weird emotion attacks her, she subconsciously hangs up and instead dials another number.

"Hello," she says when a familiar voice answers.

"Hey Donna, what's up baby?" Gina, a current, no good ass lover asks.

"Nothing much, you wanna come eat some pussy? I have had the weirdest day and need some release."

"You know I got you girl! Let me put these bad-ass kids to bed and I'm on the way!"

"Cool baby, call me when you on the way," she says, as she visualizes Gina's fine, tight ass body.

"Uh, baby I'm gonna need gas money, and my light bill is due. You think you can let me hold a bill?"

Donna smacks her lips and responds, "Yeah I can do that, just get your ass over here and don't forget yo strap nigga!"

CHAPTER SIX

Renee awakens to the confines of a box. She is shut in and can't find her way out. She can't breathe and begins to scream, then realizes that she doesn't *have* to breathe. A flood of thoughts invade her mind. She remembers, in this silence, the previous nights' occurrences.

She remembers the sweet flow of thick blood running down her throat and the incredible feeling of life course through her veins. She recalls how she sucked on Sasha's wound, slow at first and then with a need that was insatiable.

"Slow down dear one," Sasha admonished. "You can only drink to a limit with me, or we shall both perish. Be still."

Renee, feeling a new strength, only pulled her closer, wanting that which now seemed to be the only thing that mattered.

As she fed, she saw glimpses of, what, memories? She could not be sure and at that moment, really didn't care.

A jungle, Sasha clad in loincloth, a spear in hand as she tracks what? There is an animal, the image is fleeting yet Renee is sure it is a big cat of some sort. Then she sees darkness as Sasha emerges into a clearing, kill in hand.

The sounds of a mighty waterfall echo in her ears as she witnesses a man, tall in stature, float down from the trees above and land on the unsuspecting woman. There is a brief struggle and then she sees Sasha, blood upon her ebony skin, walk through the ruins of a small village. Bodies are strewn about in heaps!

Men with elaborate headdresses upon their heads, and women still clutching naked babies to their bosoms.

"Renee, this you cannot do!" Sasha whispered as she pulled forcefully away.

The beast has awakened and hunger reigns. "I need more," Renee states, her eyes a filmy rose color.

"Yes, you will feed this night…"

The image of Donna is projected from Sasha's mind. It caused the last remnant of humanness to the forefront of Renee's mind.

She bolts upright; her newfound strength sending Sasha flying across the room.

"NO! You can't, you wouldn't!" She reached out desperately, to feel Sasha's thoughts, but was no match for the stronger being.

Sasha rebounded from the dresser and landed easily on her feet. A smirk crossed her face.

"I knew I chose wisely. You already can see my thoughts? Never in my history has someone learned so quickly!"

Renee leaped across the room but found her body literally paralyzed when she reached Sasha. Something like a force field immobilized her.

She struggled to speak, "You won't touch her!" Her words came out slurred as she felt her eyes drawn to Sasha's. Unbelievably, the desire of struggle quickly turned into a ferocious need to fuck.

In her past body she would have been appalled; but in this new, stronger exhilarating form, she struggles with her conscience. The very reason of her wanting to save Donna seemed to have slipped a notch.

Sasha laughed, as she recognized Renee's desire. "I will take what I desire, as you well know. But, perhaps I will let that one live, for now," she teased, as she'd wrapped her arms around her. The desire between them awakened yet again, and moments later they were in back in bed.

Tongues explored with a desperate need unbeknownst to them both. Legs intertwined, clits touched and as Renee reached her climax, she saw stars, literally. The universe swept by her as she seemed to have come, 'out of body.' Her pleasure was so intense that she feared she really would die.

Worlds and times flashed before her, the earth itself she saw take form. From a barren wasteland to a land full of greens and blues, she watched as the moon exploded with her and crumbled into the sea. And once over, she lay in amazement, yet felt no rapid pounding of a heartbeat.

She'd taken Sasha's wonderful nipples into her mouth as new fangs pierced old flesh, Sasha cried out as she let her forever lover sip a little more of her ancient blood.

So they'd come to Sasha's lair just before dawn and Renee became familiar with her new tomb.

"Rest now and tonight I will teach you the art of the kill my love," Sasha instructed.

Renee's thirst was far from quenched but she felt a new alarm in her head: the coming of the morning sun. She forced the need to feed deep inside her mind and her last thought, before a new sleep engulfed her, was,

"I will not let her hurt Donna! I will not forget that one last part of me and before it is over, no matter how much I love her, Sasha will pay."

CHAPTER SEVEN

"Arise, my Queen," Sasha speaks, as she removes the heavy top from Renee's pristine coffin. She sits up in one fluid motion. As she moves to Sasha's side, her eyes feast upon the beautifully furnished room. Hundreds of books line a shelf devoted to the entire length of one wall.

An antique redwood desk, equipped with quill, ink, and what appears to be paper not held in the human hand since its invention, stands regally near a window. Black, crushed velvet drapes are tied back to reveal an amazing view of the Pacific Ocean.

The room boasts an array of original Van Gogh paintings, set against deep avocado walls. Matching leather sofa and loveseat sit at an angle near the door, a beautiful Persian rug bridging them.

Atop the rug sits a glass table with legs made of a substance of which Renee is unfamiliar. A fireplace, oddly set in this near tropical paradise, is aflame, giving the room a slight, stuffy feel.

Sasha takes Renee's slim hand in her own. She pulls her close and runs her tongue up the length of her neck. Renee swoons, her hunger matched only by the passion that this being brings. She lets her head fall backwards, inviting the 'kiss' yet now it feels forbidden to her somehow.

"No, not now," Sasha breathes deeply, while she runs her lips along first one earlobe then the other. She feels the familiar stiffening of her clit but moves away quickly, leaving a force of heat between them. "Tonight you feed, and not on my blood. There are worlds for us to travel, much I must show you."

"Yes, I am thirsty and can feel the night calling to me," Renee answers as she moves to the window. Sasha smiles knowingly as she admires her lover's perfect form.

"I can smell them. I feel heartbeats and sense every fear. How can that be so?" Renee questions.

"It is the heightened sense of awareness. Concentrate, can you not even feel the pulse of the mouse that scurries near the trash bin along the alley there?" Sasha asks, as she peers hundreds of feet into the darkness below. Renee allows her eyes to adjust to the dark and is delighted to learn that she can see along the beach walk, down to the townhouses, and into an alley that runs alongside thereof.

"It is absolutely amazing! Take me there," she insists, as she hones in on two lovers as they stroll along the sand.

"Come; let us feed my dearest, for the first time, together."

The window suddenly blows outward and the fragrance of the sea enters Renee's nose and gives new awakening. They fly, impossibly so, and are ten feet behind the two women as they giggle and hold hands. The moon is surrounded by a haze of fog; the 'Queen Mary' sounds her horn in the distance, giving signal to the eight o'clock hour.

Renee is tense in her excitement, remnants of her humanity fleeting as her breathing quickens.

"No baby, I don't want to go to the club! Let's go eat and take in a movie," one of the women says with laughter.

"Now Cherie, we can't back out now! The others will be waiting."

Sasha places her hand on Renee's arm to still her. She looks into her green eyes and thinks, "let's savor this pair, for they are much like us."

Renee stills her hunger and they take hands.

"Hello ladies!" Sasha calls out cheerfully. "Where's the hot spot? We are new to the area and looking to party."

Both women turn, startled from their thoughts and gasp at the two beautiful women before them.

"Oh, well, we were going down to the club at the end of the pier," the woman with the short buzz cut says.

"Yes, but I am trying to talk my wife out of that tonight!" the one with gorgeous blue eyes states. Both women seem at ease, no knowledge of their impending doom evident in their thoughts.

"My name is Cherie and this Brittany," the one with the blue eyes says, as she extends her hand to Renee.

Sasha raises an eyebrow as she senses the immediate attraction oozing from the woman.

"Nice to meet you," Renee returns, her white teeth glistening in the moonlight. The women shake hands and their touch lingers a second or two too long.

Brittany watches her wife's eyes glaze over and thinks, "What the fuck?"

Sasha catches the thought and quickly takes her hand. "I am Sasha and this is Renee. As I said, we are looking for a nice place to kick back tonight." Her eyes meet Brittany and she uses her hypnotism to still the jealous woman.

In a dazed voice Brittany replies, "Yes, come down the beach, we can all go together."

"Of course, and it will be my treat!" Sasha answers, as she gives Renee a hard look of her own.

Renee nudges close to Sasha, her eyes never leaving those of Cherie. "Oh what this will be fun! I haven't been out in a while!" she lies.

The four women continue along the beach, as the waves lap high up onto the sand. The fog makes it way heavily to the shore, blocking out the moonlight.

Sasha stiffens as they walk. *"What's the matter love?"* Renee sends to her.

"I will tear that bitch from asshole to mouthpiece if you fuck with me!"

Renee, quite amused, stifles her laughter.

"Do not fuck with me dear heart, for you know not of what you deal!" Sasha states, mind to mind, emphatically.

"It isn't what you think! I want to drain her and quickly before I lose my nerve! You are the one who wants to play!"

Sasha's eyes narrow as she smiles amicably at the two bewildered women in their presences.

"The club is just up here," Brittany states, her mind in a fog and her eyes in a daze.

Cherie looks eagerly at Sasha, "Yep, right up ahead on the left," she points at a small spot on the corner with much activity leading from the parking lot ahead and to the front entrance.

The women approach the payment booth just inside the small, crowded club.

"Four," Sasha says to the attendant behind the safety glass.

"That will be forty dollars, please."

Sasha reaches into the pocket of her black hip huggers and pulls out nothing. She seduces the attendant with her eyes and pushes air through the slot.

"Thank you!" the attendant replies, as she opens the tile and lifts the place for twenties. She inserts nothingness, her eyes a cloudy gray. "Enjoy your night at 'Claudia's on The Strand!'"

The women enter, have their wrist stamped, and are greeted by the sound of disco bumping through the speakers.

"Wow, now this is a party!" Cherie shouts above the music.

The club is wall to wall women. Strippers occupy several poles, the greedy loners at their feet. The bar is filled to capacity as Sasha leads her group to a recently deserted table. Half-empty drinks crown the table, and a coat or two litters the chairs, but in a flash Sasha makes all that go away.

"Sit here my only," she says as she escorts Renee to a chair. She looks at Brittany and Cherie, the still dazed couple, and admonishes them to sit.

"I will order our drinks."

Sasha, in black jeans made to look upon, and a lace form fitting black camisole, strolls to the bar, every eye upon her regal form. Her long curls bounce with every step, a path clearing for her as has been the case since the beginning of time.

She relishes the attention, a small smile playing upon her lips. Perfect as a woman can be, her boots clicking on the concrete floor, she glides to the bar and plants herself on a stool recently vacated.

"What can I get for you, precious?" the bartender asks a smile on her inviting, innocent lips.

"Two Daiquiris, a Gin and Tonic, and a French Connection," Sasha states, as she bats her unusually long lashes.

"Coming right up Cutie!" the bartender replies, her eyes focused and intent on Sasha. She turns to mix the drinks and Sasha, for the first time, is puzzled. She turns quickly to look back at Renee, when suddenly, a form known to her for over one hundred years, is there!

"Sasha! Queen of everything unholy! Welcome to my space!" a voice states.

The entity before her is Angela! The one she loved and killed before the time of the holocaust! She is imposing! Beautiful, with her light flawless skin and straight red hair! The sight of her after all this time, takes Sasha's breath away!

The shock of her leaves no room for words! She sits, the bartender now shows fangs, the activity of the room moves in slow motion! Now Sasha sees what she has missed before: the bouncer shows sharp fangs! The bartender! Three dancers with eyes made of blood! The Fucking Deejay!

"Angela! Well, well! I thought I had banished you to the underworld!" Sasha says in the quiet of their own time: the humans of this fiasco seem to be moving along as if nothing is amiss.

Angela wipes the sweat from her brow. "I have waited a long time for you my maker! I had the strangest feelings tonight upon my awakening! I smelled you coming," she whispers, as she moves slowly around her still sitting and stunned maker.

"It's been a long time Ang, too long in fact! The last time I saw you I engulfed you with fire! Now how did you ever get out of that? Umm, you never cease to amaze me!" Sasha says, as she turns to get Renee in her view.

"Yes, there was a little issue with fire as I recall. Yuri," she says to the bartender, "Get me the usual!"

"Sure thing boss, a Bloody Mary is just what the occasion calls for," Yuri responds.

"Angela, I see you still can't resist giving low life's the gift!" Sasha says through clinched teeth.

"That was a problem between us wasn't it *'Queen?'* The demon asks, as she looks over to Renee.

"Now she is pretty! Is that who has taken my place in your bed and heart? I am offended!"

Sasha stands suddenly, a new quickness even for her. She stands face to face with the one she despises. "This is between you and me Angela! If you even *think* about it, I will…"

"You will what? I have had years to gain strength and knowledge! Her fangs are suddenly extended as she reaches for the Queen of Darkness!

CHAPTER EIGHT

Donna sits up, her body used and abused. She feels everything she has ever desired after a night of lovemaking, wait, FUCKING is a better term. She knows that Gina is using her, but for now it is okay.

Something has always been missing but she is far from being a fool. The comfort of a woman is better than no comfort at all, and with that, she can live.

Even Renee thinks she is a fool, but she knows better. A friend is something hard to come by, and she knows the essence of Renee: slow to anger, easy to talk to, even easier to get something from. The Lord only knows the things they have been through! Oh but there's a change in the wind! She feels something is very wrong.

There is something brewing, but if only she could remember! She keeps seeing these damn birds, and what? Blood or some shit? Whatever is going on *somebody* has got it twisted! Because with her last breathe she will defend the one true friend she has!

"Hey baby!" Gina says, as she comes from the bathroom, her body and hair dripping water! A towel wrapped around her vanilla body, only makes Donna's heart skip a beat. She dry's her hair, her breast dangling like only a child bearers' can. The sight is enough to drive Donna insane, yet...

"Hey baby, you got me sleeping late! You know I got shit to do!" Donna says.

Gina cringes inside, wishing she could just get her damn hundred dollars and shake a spot! The pussy is good, but damn! The kids' daddy is coming over tonight and that is really her true love!

"I'm leaving baby! You know them damn kid's love their oatmeal and mama got to feed them!"

Donna looks suspiciously at this chick and smirks, realizing that oatmeal if for fucking breakfast! Just to fuck with her she says, "I got the money for your bill baby. I was just thinking we could go out tonight before you go home, hell we done slept the whole day away so what's another couple of hours gonnna hurt?

Gina stares at the heavy woman on the bed and weighs her options: Tyrone who hasn't paid child support in years, or Donna, who isn't so bad, for a few more hours. "I'm game baby!" she smiles.

"Now that's what I want to hear! Let's go to 'Claudia's! They are jumping tonight, Karaoke and shit." Donna extends her hands and invites Gina back to bed.

Gina goes to her, less than willingly. They embrace, the scent off last night's lovemaking engulfing their noses. Sheets array, hair tasseled, they fuck again. A need exempt from time, space or circumstance, just a need to be! And they come together, a need bigger than themselves. Tongues touch, hands explore, legs and hips search, all simply for the meaning of love.

And when it is over and the fog rolls in, they both, no matter the circumstance, are sated and ready to venture into the night.

"Wait what the hell was that? Donna asks, as they approach the entrance to the club.

Gina pauses, the screams from within greets her ears. For the first time, since her child was born, feet first, she is afraid. Something smashes against, perhaps a wall?

The very foundation shakes! Shimmering sights, lightening flashes, colors never witnessed before! The women stand outside, eyes wide in astonishment!

"Renee!" Donna screams her voice shrill in the night.

Gina looks at her part time lover, "who the hell is Re…" the words are barely out before Donna heaves her 200 hundred pounds through the door!

The cautious side of Gina forces her to run back to her car parked across the street near the water. She hauls ass as the sounds of screams, chaos, and shit literally hitting the fan!

"Oh my Lawd," Donna exclaims, never stopping to wonder how the hell she knows Renee is inside.

As she rushes through the door, her body stiffens at the sight of carnage; Bodies are askew on the floor, blood drips from the walls. The music mocks her every turn. The bartender stands, head missing, pouring a fathom drink. Her head, mouth wide open and teeth snapping, moves sluggishly across the bar, and pops down to the ground.

"What the hell?" Donna exclaims, as she kicks the head away from her.

She searches for the validation of her sanity: "Is that a fucking Vampire on the pole snacking on a *human arm?*

And is that a bitch crawling along the ceiling? What in God's name is fucking happening? "

Donna scans the room, the cross draped around her neck in hand. *"Turn to the left,"* a voice says in her inner heart, and in doing so, she fends off a *thing* that has glided across the room, with, Lord, have mercy, fangs?

The symbol of all she has grown to trust and love touches the thing and it immediately turns to dust.

"Oh my Sweet Jesus," she says, as the remnants of her attacker falls to the floor. Donna breathes in deeply and steps further inside.

The deejay, a floor above but in plain view, continues to spin a Donna Summer's classic. Teeth that seem to be way too long, drips what appears to be blood. Three or four bodies lay at her feet, all dead.

She spies Donna below, and suddenly flees through an open window. Donna moves hesitantly through the room scared out of her mind, yet somehow she knows that her friend is here somewhere.

A group of tables greet her, and although she notices no movement, there is a woman who stands on the small Karaoke floor, holding a mike. There is a look of stun on her face as she surveys the carnage.

Her white dress and face are maroon stained as she stares at a monitor, the words of her song unaffected by whatever has occurred.

Donna approaches her cautiously and decides that she is human.

"Honey," Donna states gently as she removes the mike from her hand, "You know what the hell is going on?"

The woman, Tanisha her name, seems to awaken as if from a dream.

"Okay I'm leaving now; I need to check the stew I have cooking in the crock pot."

She gives the mike to Donna staggers out the door.

The smell is stifling as Donna places the mike on a nearby table. She notices two women, apparently a couple, gripping one another in death. One, her hair cut low, and the other, blue eyes amazingly inviting, even in death, have the look of surprise on their faces. Both their throats are ripped out, yet there is no blood evident.

"What the hell happened here?" she asks the empty room as tears begin to stream down her cheeks.

"I AM WHAT HAPPENED, CHILD OF GOD!"

Donna turns, cross in hand and recognizes the woman who assaulted her while in her car. She is beautiful! She is the woman of every human's desire. Donna exhales, as she tries to keep her sanity and purpose in check.

"I know you!" she exclaims, never taking her hand from her silver cross.

Sasha grins, seductively as she eyes the taboo in this one's hand. "Of course you do! I am ALL. Do you not see me in your dreams?"

The will of Donna slips, as she sees herself lost in the form before her. Her sex is aroused and the cross slips carelessly from her fingertips.

Sasha slinks nearer, her eyes never lowering to meet her victim's. She concentrates her will, lets it flow dangerously out to this women who clearly has the mark of God, her only true nemesis, upon her.

"Come to me and I will give you life that you have only dreamt of!" she says, her hips seductively swaying as she draws closer still. The room is hot, the smell of blood in the air. Donna digs deep; the thought of Renee fills her mind as she takes a step backwards.

"Where is Renee? I know she is here and I will kill your ass if you have done anything to hurt her!"

Sasha pauses, as she wets her glistening lips. With one hand she gestures the length of the room.

"Do you see her here, among this death? No, she is covered by me and will live until this world is dead! Believe and trust that day draws near, but I can give you life everlasting!

"You need only ask. Women," Sasha continues, her hair moving with a wind of its own, "they use and abuse you! How your heart would leap at the sight of all those who have harmed you on a stake made of wood!"

Donna scans the room again, the last movement of some sort of life stops and there is silence. Her hand now down by her side, her throat dry and rancid.

"What I want is to see Renee, anything else if the last thing on my mind! You fine and all that but fuck you!"

Donna reaches inside of her shirt and finds the cross again. She pulls it up and out as Sasha draws near. The sight causes her to cover her eyes and squeal as if burned! Her fangs extend and for an instant, she appears ancient! Wrinkles form on her face and her hair flashes grey!

Then, so quickly that Donna thinks she may have imagined it, Sasha is once again a striking twenty-five year old woman! Donna stares; her mouth hangs open in shock.

Then Renee is there, her face glowing and mouth smeared with what? Blood or some shit?

Donna doesn't know what to do. Did her friend just fly down from the raptors?

"SASHA!" she screams, the fury evident on her lovely face. "I will abide with you for eternity but will leave you if you do this! She is my friend!"

Sasha looks upon the one she has chosen and back to the one she wishes to destroy. Her teeth ease back into their gums and she raises that signature eyebrow.

"Now this is truly a dilemma! I have walked into a trap, met my old fledgling, banished that bitch and some of her dominion into the night, **and** managed to summon the fucking police, which will be here shortly I might add! Yet all you care about is this human who offers you nothing! She screams at Renee.

Renee moves between the two women and smiles at Sasha. "I am yours, but this one you cannot have. It is the will of the most High and you feel it as well as I do. Let's go I will satisfy your hunger! She you can't touch! Get use to it!"

Sasha rears back her head and howls. The sound is deafening and Donna struggles to cover her ears.

"Renee?" Donna whispers, after the assault on her ears, mind and spirit subsides.

Renee turns and looks, with sympathy upon her friend.

"I love you Donna, and know you must be confused. Just understand that I am okay and will let nothing harm you, ever!"

Sasha sees red at this statement, but controls herself, mainly due to the cross the bitch holds in her hand. If not for that, she would have consummated her feast by now.

"Renee, what, what are you?"

Renee shakes her head, "I have been damned by my lust Donna! I am ashamed to stand before you. You have to leave now!"

"NO! Are you insane? Renee, it's me, your friend! I love you and I am not leaving without you!"

Renee walks dangerously close to her friend and the cross. Sasha frowns, her breath caught in her throat.

"Listen to me Donna, I have chosen this and can't explain right now. Go now and I promise I will come to you, when I can, and explain."

Donna places the impending fate of her friend inside her shirt, leaving nothing between them.

"Please Lord protect me," she whispers as she steps into her friend's arms.

CHAPTER NINE

Sasha watches as jealousy settles in her heart. She sees the bitch put the cross inside her shirt. A gleam shines in her eye.

"Oh what a fucking night this has been! Sasha thinks. Her past lover, decades thought gone, reappears and with the scum of the earth no less! She'd reached and caught that Bitch just before her strong hands could wrap around her neck.

The flimsy assed bartender had her fangs just at her neck, but oh! They underestimated her! She'd knocked that bitches head off, with one swift blow, laughing as it ricocheted against the bar.

Angela, however, was stronger! She tried to grab Sasha by the hair as she'd reached back to strike Yuri. She was a second too late, forgetting how fast Sasha could move!

Then, from the corner of her eye she spied Renee flying at her, the beautiful contours of her face twisted in fury! Rinella pissed but far from stupid, loosened the grip and fled out of the door, disappearing into the night.

A group of her dominion managed to feed upon the unsuspecting crowd before fleeing. The two women they picked up earlier were among those unlucky enough to choose this club tonight: a stripper nearby took advantage of the chaos and ripped their throats to shreds.

So now she stands, as her lover embraces a human enshrouded with the 'Grace of God!' Never fear and she does not, for she has gone up against that entity before and millennium later, still stands.

Renee tenses as Donna steps into her arms. The cross separated only by a thin layer of cloth, and she can feel it as it struggles to touch and destroy her! She quickly releases Donna.

Sasha she can see from the corner of her eye, and she knows enough to understand that she is no match for her just yet. With this heart that no longer beats, she still loves her friend, and realizes that Sasha will happily tear Donna to shreds, her intense jealousy already known.

"Donna, go home," Renee advises, the sounds of sirens filling the air.

"Oh, no you don't! I have seen some shit in my time but this is nuts! This is like waking up in one of your scary ass books! What happened to you Renee? It was her wasn't it?" she asks as she turns towards Sasha.

Renee steps away and goes to embrace her lover, with hopes this will still her.

"We have to get out of here! I can't explain now," Renee admonishes.

Sasha wraps her arms firmly around Renee and extends her fangs. To Donna she hisses, "Let's make this one our slave my love! Let me give her to you, in death, as a gift."

"No Sasha, let's just go. I need to feed before the sun rises," she sends to Sasha's mind, along with the image of her lips smeared with blood.

To Donna, Sasha whispers, "We shall meet again and I sooo look forward to it!"

Renee looks deep into Donna's eyes and *wills* her to get the hell out of here before she's on the cover of every newspaper in the country, accused of being involved in this carnage. She is indeed a quick study, for she sees Donna's eyes glaze over and she sends one last thought: *"These things you have seen, you will not remember Donna! I will come to you, GO!"*

Donna opens her mouth to speak, but before one word is uttered, the pair is out the door like a swift, cold, autumn breeze.

The cold night air wraps around Donna like a shroud as she walks along Pacific Coast Highway at two in the morning. She feels dazed and can only think a single thought: "That damn Gina left me stranded!" She vaguely remembers entering the club but everything after that point is hazy. She does however, know that her ass is walking in the middle of the night with at least fifteen miles to go and Gina's ass drove her out tonight!

"Now why did that bitch leave? Especially when I didn't give her the hundred…" Donna smiles at the remembrance and her head does clear. She reaches and pulls out her cell phone.

"Yes, I need a taxi at the corner of PCH and Cherry."

"Ok, be there in about five minutes," the dispatcher answers.

Donna spots a bus stop bench and takes a seat as the fog thickens. She hears a multitude of sirens to the south of her, near the club she has recently abandoned, but nothing registers in her mind. She toys with her cell phone and decides to call that lying assed Gina.

"Hello?" a scruffy ass male voice answers.

"Yes, may I speak to Gina?" she asks.

"Who this be?" The male voice answers.

Donna smirks, knowing this has to be the kids' father. She feels the familiar stir of disappointment but it is quickly stilled by the yellow car which swoops to the curb.

"Never mind, I'll call later," she states, and snaps her phone closed before he can respond.

She enters the backdoor of the taxi and relishes the warmth within.

"9766 W. 218th street," she directs, as she closes the door and leans her head against the comfortable headrest.

The driver pulls off and adjusts the rearview mirror to look directly at the woman in the backseat. Had Donna's eyes been open she would have noticed the driver cast no reflection in the mirror. Unfortunately, she does not see and doesn't feel the car turn south when the driver should clearly be headed west.

Renee is on the wave of yet another intensely satisfying orgasm. She looks down at Sasha, watches her lick the tip of her clit, her fangs playfully nipping and tongue probing. Their eyes meet and a smile touches the corner of Renee's lips.

"Ooh this bitch is good! She can suck and fuck like no other! If she hadn't pissed me off and tricked me, I would love her for a lifetime…"

She lays back and enjoys the pleasure given her, hunger sated and nothing to do but enjoy the pleasure until the sun meets the horizon a few of hours hence.

Renee flexes her buttocks, extends her arms over her head and curls her toes as her maker laps every ounce of fluid her touch has produced. She is okay for now, as she experiences sex like never before. There haven't been many lovers in her life, although she has had her share of offers. She knows she is what some would call 'gorgeous,' but that means nothing to her. She has taken a few lovers but for the most part, has been a loner.

This suits her, or has. What does this new life mean? Earlier, although she had been mad as hell at Sasha, when she sensed the danger around her, she'd kept an eye on the Stud by the bar. So when the bitch reached out for Sasha's throat, she'd just reacted. No thought entered her mind, and the anger she'd felt flew out the window. Red is the color that flashed in front of her eyes and killing that whore was all she could think.

Does that mean she is bound to Sasha in some strange way? Or does it mean she really loves her? This new body and foreign feeling has her perturbed. However, at this moment she wishes nothing more than to cum over and over again before she slumbers at the upcoming sunrise.

"This one is special," Sasha thinks as she runs a long nail along Renee's thigh.

"Ahh," the sound escapes Renee's lips as blood begins to seep from her wounds. She is mesmerized as she watches Sasha roll the fluid along her tongue. Playfully she makes shallow cuts up and down her tense body. Her fangs invade places no teeth should touch, yet she is Sasha and there are no limits to her wanting.

Suddenly she flips Renee over, her back exposed. Teeth to flesh she rends more skin, her excitement matched with eagerness to achieve her own orgasm. She feels the mounting pressure but chooses to hold out and let her love show through discipline. Down her spine she drags her teeth, the taste of blood only helping to ensure something quite extraordinary to come.

No longer able to contain that which has mounted, Renee turns her blood stained body over. "Come here love," Renee directs, as she pulls Sasha's perfect body to her own. The kiss is sensual, as it has been from the beginning. Deep, Sasha forces her tongue, as she reaches and tries to discover the essence of this being that has made her weak.

The muscles of her stomach tighten, her thighs vibrate, she gasps as she touches her own throbbing sex to her lover's and is ashamed as she screams out her name in orgasmic ecstasy.

Sunrise draws nearer still and all is perfect before the time of dark sleep. Renee lays her head upon the breast of a still heart. She breathes in all that is, that was, and that is destined to be. Suddenly Sasha sits up, Renee flung aside like a ragdoll.

"What...?"

"Shhh! something is amiss!" Sasha whispers, her ear cocked towards the window.

Renee looks perplexed. She studies her lovers face, concentrates her will and searches Sasha's mind.

"What is it baby?"

In her mind's eye, Sasha sees the taxi and Donna screaming for her life. The undead driver reaches for her,

Donna's struggle to bring out the dreaded cross from beneath her lilac colored shirt. As she prevails and this fledgling turns to dust, the door is thrown open and she is surrounded by a mob. At its head is Angela, death in her eye.

"Now, now, no need to fight; I have no intentions on hurting you!"

Donna holds the cross out before her. She is appalled by what she sees: beings in their raw state before her. "What the fuck is this?" she wonders as she stares, mouth agape. A whole lot of motherfucker's looking like some shit out of '*The Night of the Living Dead!*'

The only one even resembling a human being is a fine ass bitch, but Donna is not fooled. She holds the cross for dear life and eases her way out of the cab.

She sees the ones in front back away from the symbol she holds. "Oh, you motherfucker's don't like this I see!"

Angela locks her eyes with Donna's and summons centuries of power and sends to her, *"put that away my dear and come to me. I will make you my queen! I shall give you beauty beyond all that you have ever desired."*

She wills Donna to pull the cross free and just as she licks her lips in anticipation of the kill, that bitch Sasha swoops from the sky and wields that damn sword of hers! The same sword that nearly ended Angela's dark life!

Sasha, quicker than anything most of these fledglings have ever seen, cuts and dices through them like a fine mist. In the blink of an eye, most of the demons are dust or shrinking away in fear. Angela howls in fury!

"Damn you Sasha! Do you know how many years it takes to gather an army like this?" she screams, her fangs extended, her eyes red and bulging.

Sasha lands lightly near Donna, who shakes her head to clear her mind and struggles to keep it from slipping at the sight she has just witnessed. She looks at the symbol of her faith in her hand, chain broken, and feels shame.

For one split second, she'd entertained throwing the chain to the ground and going to the demon.

"Now Angela," Sasha laughs, "an army is usually strong, not these weak beings you picked up out of the gutter! You mock the very reason of our existence! You are impulsive and seek your own destruction. Did you forget why I banished you from my fold?"

Angela takes a step towards the two women but hesitates as Sasha twirls the sword about.

"I have made an oath to destroy you Sasha, and destroy you I will!"

"If you say so, but it shall not be here, not this night. So tell me what you planned to do with this one?" she asks, as she nods towards Donna.

"Oh, you don't think I feel what she means to your bitch? I saw the nice little scene in the club. My club and haven that you have fucked up by the way! Years I have been there and in five minutes you took that away. You and that new fuck of yours will pay! As for this one, I plan to make her my dog, and you better believe I will!"

Sasha laughs on the deserted street. She senses the rising of the sun and decides there is not time to toy with Angela.

"Well I as your maker say again, not this night. Now, we can finish this game another time or you can stand here and burn in the morning sun, the choice is yours. As for me and the human, we are out." With that, Sasha grabs Donna, sure to keep away from the symbol, and in a flash, they are gone from that place.

CHAPTER TEN

"No! Stay here my love! You are not quick enough! The sun draws near and I will not risk you burning before me! I will handle this!" Sasha shouted. Renee was confused and sick with fear at the thought of Sasha going out so close to dawn. The back and forth between loving and hating her was driving her mad!

"Then at least tell me what the fuck is happening! Why can't I read your thoughts right now?"

"Because you are young my dear, and in the throngs of sex your awareness is down. It happens in the beginning, do not worry, over time you will grow stronger," Sasha stated as she neared the window.

"Sasha! What would make you go out so close to the rising sun?"

"Angela, at this moment, seeks to take your little friend into her fold. Is that what you want?"

Renee looked on in horror. "Donna? She has Donna?"

"Yes, and under any other circumstance I wouldn't give a fuck! Angela, however, shall not take that which I seek, ever again. Also, you have seduced me this night and so as my thanks I will save this *'friend'* of yours. Does this not please you? Now let me go before it is too late!"

"Sasha, don't hurt her. I swear to stay with you always, just don't do anything to her. I don't want this for her."

Sasha, eyes turned crimson at the affection in Renee's voice, smirked and nodded her agreement.

With that, she was gone, a blur in the sky. Renee stood at the window not quite knowing what to do. Confused, she went to the bed to wait. She tried desperately to reach out for Sasha's mind but could see only darkness.

Renee had never been a religious person. Having grown up in an abusive home, faith was something she'd given up on a long time ago. As a child she'd prayed to God to rescue her, but those prayers went unanswered.

As a result, she labored through childhood as best she could. The only pleasures and love she received came from the many books she submerged herself into.

She read anything she could get her hands on! She loved words and so naturally began to create her own worlds. She began writing stories every chance she got, and soon began to live inside her creations.

Her imagination helped her survive a mother and father who ignored her except only at times when they had no other choice but to acknowledge her presence.

She often heard them refer to her as 'their little accident', and it wasn't until she was older, that she understood what that meant. They were almost middle aged when she was conceived, and they resented her for interrupting their carefully planned out life.

Shortly after she'd graduated from High School, she'd submitted a short story to a national mystery magazine, and was surprised when they published it! Thereafter, for the next few years, her work was regularly published. Her earnings were not enough to live off, so she worked various temporary jobs.

Then her parents were killed in an automobile accident and she'd inherited a substantial sum of money and the family home. Not having to work to support herself, she settled down and focused on her first novel.

It was a huge success! She wrote in the horror genre, and six books and millions of fans later, she had become quite wealthy. Renee enjoyed success, but was a loner so never fully experienced its pleasures. She'd been comfortable but lonely and with Sasha's new 'dark gift,' she felt a new found freedom that no amount of money could buy.

She still, however, promises herself that no matter how much she changes, she will suffer no harm to come to Donna. She doesn't know if this is normal for one of her kind, but she could still *feel* the love and compassion that she'd always felt for her friend.

How much would she change over time? She wondered. Already she knew that she could kill easily in order to quench the gnawing need that nagged at her insides. Perhaps it came easily because of her many years of writing of nothing but murder and mayhem.

These and many thoughts flew through her mind as she sat and waited for Sasha's return.

"Put that fucking thing away!" Sasha admonishes as she throws Donna heavily to the floor of her apartment. Donna crawls into a corner and refuses to put the cross away.

"I know you!" she whispers to Sasha. "Of course you do and stop saying that!" Sasha removes the veil from Donna's mind and gives her back all of her recent memories.

"Oh my God it's YOU! The old fearless Donna is back and she stands. "Where is Renee?"

Sasha rears her head back and laughs loud enough to wake the building. "Sentimental assed human beings drive me fucking nuts! She is as safe as you are thanks to me! Now the sun rises and I am stuck here with you! You better be thankful that I fed well tonight!"

Sasha begins to move through the spacious apartment, seeking a safe place to slumber.

"What the hell you think you doing?" Donna asks, careful not to become too bold for she remembers that her faith slipped earlier and the cross could be relinquished just as quickly as it could be yielded as a weapon.

"Listen you piece of shit! It is only because I love Renee that you still stand in my terrible presence! Do not anger me further. Now I saved your life and now I must sleep. I will be your guest today and if you even dare come near me while I slumber, I will risk all to rip out your fucking guts and feed them to your mother! Who, by the way lives in San Diego?"

Donna stops suddenly, the picture of her mother being fed her intestines very vivid in her mind.

"What you need me to do?" she asks, real fear in her voice.

"I need darkness, perfect blackness. And you will not come near me!"

Donna looks at this amazingly beautiful woman, a big silver sword sheathed behind her back. Her tight ass pants hugging wonderful thighs, and breast high and mighty. Donna looks away, perplexed by how quickly her anger and fear has turned to desire. Sasha smirks for she *knows* the look.

"A closet of some sort?" she asks. "Hey! This is serious child! The sun draws neigh!"

Donna allows herself to trust this woman, slightly, because she did save her life.

"Okay, in the bedroom, my closet is dark I suppose and no one will go in there."

"Oh of that I am sure! You did have a woman here recently, I smell her. Not many others though," Sasha teases.

"Look, you want the fucking closet or not? Because I really don't care what the sun does to you! I just want to know what you did to Renee and where she is, and by the look in your eyes this sun shit is really serious for you!"

Sasha exposes her fangs and hisses at the woman. Donna shrinks away in fear, her eyes as wide as saucers.

"Take me to the damn closet before I forget myself!"

She is led to the bedroom, the sun already showing its glory behind the drapes. Sasha slinks along a wall and makes her way to the closet door. Donna flings it open to reveal a spacious space filled with clothes, shoes, and the usual shit that fills a woman's space.

"This will have to do," Sasha mumbles to herself. "I can't believe I am in this position!" she thinks. Never in the history of her existence has she put herself at risk for anyone or anything.

"Okay, I must sleep, and remember what I said. I AM SASHA QUEEN OF ALL!" to emphasize this, she changes to her true form, that of an old ancient thing. Her beauty fades and she is suddenly over three thousand years old!

Donna shrieks and faints to the floor.

Sasha laughs as the heavy form hits the floor. She changes back and enters the closet. It is indeed dark and faces south. The sun will not touch this place, and that bitch better not disturb her slumber. Suddenly she feels Renee reach out to her and she blocks her mind!

"Let her suffer this night! Then she will be obliged to follow my orders when I return," Sasha thinks. She is indeed manipulative, how else could she have survived this long? Sasha rips all the clothes from their hangars and buries herself deep beneath them and sleeps.

CHAPTER ELEVEN

Donna wakes suddenly; fear enshrouds her like a blanket. It is past noon and she fells disoriented.

"What the hell?" she asks the silent room. As she sits up the closet looms before her.

"Oh fuck me! Is there a fucking old ass Vampire in there?" The answer to this she knows to be true. She backs away, her ass burning on the carpet. The phone rings and scares the shit out of her!

Donna inches her way to the nightstand and answers.

"Hello?"

Gina's voice greets her. "Umm, hey baby, just calling to make sure you are okay!"

Donna cringes at the chipper, fake tone. She remembers this bitch fleeing the scene and leaving her to fucking die!

"Yeah I'm cool. You sure took off in a hurry!"

"Yeah, well, that club is all over the fucking news today and I still can't believe we were there! The police are saying that fifty dead people were in there! Girl what you see when you went in?"

Donna pulls her stiff body onto the bed, her eyes never leaving the closet door.

"I don't know what you talking about, I didn't see shit!"

"What? Girl they offering a big reward if anybody knows something, and I was thinking, hell we should get some of that money!"

Donna feels sickened at this money hungry motherfucker and wonders how she should handle this. It is obvious that the chick in the closet turned Renee into something unholy, yet the bitch did save her from being that other one's midnight snack, or worse.

"Listen Gina, I think you better leave this shit alone! There are things out there that I didn't even believe in. Let it go and don't tell anyone you went there. Take my advice or some shit may visit you in the night!"

"Well Tyrone said…"

Donna remembers him having answered the phone last night.

"Tyrone? I thought you weren't fucking with his worthless ass anymore?"

"I'm not honey! He just thinks…"

Donna gets angry quick and returns, "listen, you better take my advice and leave it alone! Now I have to go and you know what? Don't call me again Gina because you must think I'm crazy!" With that she slams down the phone.

She stares at the closet, the temptation to open the door and look inside is overwhelming, but the picture of her poor old mother being served her guts is equally overwhelming and so she grabs a pillow and holds on to it for dear life as she settles down to wait for the sun to set.

"I will destroy that black bitch!" Angela screams into the hollows of the cavern into which she has taken refuge. In the cliffs of San Pedro there are caves and although this is a major downgrade, at the coming of the morning it is here she has fled.

Years ago she dwelt here, before her venture into the club scene. Back before her pockets where filled and she was still, after years, recovering from the damaged Sasha inflicted upon her.

"Come my darling, let us go feed," Dahlia, her current lover states.

"Feed? You think of feeding while that bitch roams the earth destroying my shit?" Angela sails across the room and suddenly her fangs are buried deep into Dahlia's neck! The poison she drains and spits upon the earth as she rips her head from her body. Just as quickly as her anger is arisen, so does her regret.

"Fuck! Look what you made me do! Why a bitch can't just shut the fuck up!" she screams as she tosses the head out of the cave and sends it sailing into the ocean. Her tears are uncontrollable as she paces to and fro.

The few fledglings, who escaped Sasha's sword, slink into the corners. They are ravished but know better than to mention feeding.

"I swear on all that is demonic! I will find her and that new bitch of hers and turn them to dust!" she shouts, as her curls flow behind her, her beautiful skin exposed in her nakedness. "How dare she interfere with me? And my beloved club! There is no way we can abide there! The police, the goddamn media! She will pay for this I promise you."

Angela's small breast heave with each short, angry breath she takes. The others watch from the shadows, daring not to move and exact the same fate that Dahlia so shortly ago met.

She stops and regains her composure, the difference on her face like night and day. She smiles, a plan forming in her mind. She strolls to her clothes and slips them on.

"Come by darlings, let's feed on the unsuspecting! I think this will make me forget that I just destroyed my lover of the past three decades in haste. She steps over the ashes of Dahlia and steps out to meet the smell of her beloved ocean.

"Yes my queen, let us go into the night. We will find this 'Sasha' and tear her apart with our bare hands!" states Rinella, one of Angela's many lovers. Ah, but Dahlia was her mate and the thought of her actions makes her madder still!

"Rinella, I have a job for you my most trusted servant."

"Anything for you!" she answers anticipation of satisfaction upon her face.

"I know my sweet. After the feed I want you to find where she lives, the human. It has to be near for there would be little time for Sasha to make it in before sunrise. Find her and I will reward you most exceedingly."

"I vow to find the human! I will die before I disappoint you my love!" Rinella states emphatically.

"Good! Now off into the night we go. I thirst and need blood to clear my thoughts! We will need to acquire a new place to rest. I want that bitch as my familiar. She will be the new one to do my daytime bidding."

The group of Vampyre exits the caves and flies down to the shore. The moon is a wink in the sky, the night fog having cleared, and they stroll along searching for tonight's feast. Angela floats along, the perfect plan of revenge formulated in her mind.

"Donna has not moved all day. Her bladder is full, her mouth dry and she is hungry as fuck! Yet in this spot she has lay all day. At dusk, the door flies open and her heart is in her throat! "This bitch is the shit!" Donna thinks, as she can't help but desire her. She emerges; long hair tussled, which only adds to her appeal.

"You obeyed me! Perhaps there is hope for you yet, human!" Sasha says, as she nears the bed.

Donna notices that this bitch looks hungry and reaches over to the nightstand where the cross and broken chain lay.

"No need for that, I made a promise to my beloved to leave you be, for now."

Donna somehow believes her and yet doesn't like that, 'for now,' bullshit.

"Where is she? Take me to her please! I need to talk to her."

"No fucking way! You are alive, be happy with that. Renee belongs to me from now until eternity. Do not tempt me, for I will snuff your pathetic life out like a flame!"

Sasha moves to the window and throws it open. "Ah, the night is here and I thirst!" To Donna she states, "Be thankful this night, for I could drain you here and now, no matter that you hold that damn cross like a shield!

Remember this: I am ALL, older than the generations of your ancestry. I have battled your God and hundreds of others. I have lived through famine, plague, wars and natural disasters. I will BE forever and there is no one more powerful that SASHA!

Even Lilith, who came before Eve, was destroyed by this very sword! So don't not fuck with me or mine! Forget Renee, she is no longer on your human level for I have given her of ME.

She has drunk the blood of everlasting life and I will lay me down before I let her go. Each morning you wake to your miserable life, thank SASHA QUEEN OF DARKNESS for every breath you take!"

With that, she is gone out of the fourth story window, leaving Donna to stare after her in terror and amazement.

CHAPTER TWELVE

"Where were you?" Renee questions as Sasha flies in through the open window. She tosses her sword aside and strips herself of clothing.

"Sasha?" Renee follows her through the apartment, mesmerized by her long flowing hair. One moment she wishes to reach out and drag her by it, the next she longs to be wrapped inside of it.

"Sasha!" She screams, "What happened? I nearly lost my mind worrying..."

Suddenly Sasha turns her eyes aflame.

"Worried about me or your human bitch?" she questions.

Renee raises an eyebrow, her fangs exposed. "What do you think? The sun has set and I am here. Not at Donna's, not out feeding, but here!"

Sasha softens, her rage receding. She smiles at the anger in Renee. This turns her on and she remembers why she has chosen her.

"I have been buried in your friends' closet, trying not to turn to ash. Does this answer your question my dear?"

Renee allows herself an inner sigh. She can tell from the look in Sasha's dancing eyes that she has not devoured Donna. She is relieved and tries to mask this from her mind. Sasha, she has discovered, is truly not to be fucked with and so to divert her from these thoughts, she ventures, "Let's feed my darling and then let's make love." She walks to and takes Sasha's naked form in her arms.

The all knowing in Sasha is aware and so she is not fooled by Renee, yet she loves her and will bide her time. She embraces that which she so desires, however, the need to feed must be dealt with first.

"Yes, let us hunt, your lesson was not fulfilled. Then we must discuss Angela for she will not be satisfied until she proves her point. She cannot harm me, yet through my love for you, she can possibly destroy me."

"Ahh, you are quite the beauty! I think I shall give you the gift!" Angela whispers into the face of the frightened woman.

"Please, don't. I'll do anything you ask. Just don't kill me."

"The acceptance to the invitation and this pleases me!" Angela responds and sinks her sharp teeth into dark flesh. Her victim thrashes beneath her and this adds to her brutal excitement. She feels a firm breast in her hand, smells a cheap perfume, and sees visions of all the victim has known, as the hot liquid fills every fiber of her being! What was once, dead, vibrates with power!

The tasting of human fresh flesh gives the Vampyre a temporary feeling of *humanness*! Life forces itself through their veins, and even, for a split second, the heart beats. This is Angela's fix. She lives for this moment. To her discredit, she tries to hold on and in her folly, stops, then gives back.

This time is no different. She pulls away, and at the last moment cuts into her own flesh, and draws the 'dark gift.' To the woman she feeds this blood. With, little resistance, Lola Imogene Sheffield, drinks. At the moment of conception she eagerly takes life, for she is lukewarm and this means nothing to her.

The woman, who before, was simply out to take a stroll along the beach, accepts her fate. For, "I would rather live, than to die," she thinks, before a strength she never thought possible, overwhelms her.

The uncontrollable jerking of her body brings Lola to. She screams! Something renders her body into a state of shock and she feels her toes stiffen. The transformation is paralyzing. Limbs stuck in mid-motion, the anticipation in the eyes of those around her, penetrating. Yet Lola is only aware of Angela. The blood upon her lips, the gleam in her eye.

All is still as Angela laughs like a kid in a candy store.

Angela rears her head back and howls in her excitement. The full moon shines down upon the group, the newest fledging stands and looks about in wonderment. Lola stands and rises above the sand as she tests levitation.

Her fangs extend, unusually long and with her tongue she feels the tips. "Ah, I am WHOLE!" she exclaims, and the others take an uneasy step backwards.

"Come to me now for in you I see victory over those who have caused me loss," Angela directs.

Lola hisses and flies into her maker's arms. They kiss; a bloody tearing of lips and rendering of flesh that heals before the session is complete.

Lola feels an excitement in her loins like nothing she has felt before. Never has she been with another woman, hell, truth be told, she'd never been laid by a man either! Lola is one of the unlucky 'plain Jane's of the world. She also has a very bad disposition and is generally not a nice person.

She thrashes her hips wildly to meet Angela's own and suddenly they roll along the sand and seek fulfillment in one another.

"Hey, what ya'll doing down there?" a voice asks from the dark.

Angela sends to Rinella, *"take care of this for my orgasm is near."*

Rinella looks upon the one she loves and the new fledgling with hate in her eyes, yet she is quickly upon the unsuspecting owner of the voice. With her hatred she rips the man's throat out, not bothering to catch the blood before it dies in the air. She rips tears and claws to release the jealousy that has rendered her blind.

"It is supposed to be me!" she thinks as she uses her bare hands to tear the head from this being and casts it

upon the sand. *"Oh I will have my vengeance! I, who have been loyal these many years, will no longer be second! In her folly she has angered me and I will make sure this lover she enjoys no more!"*

"That's ENOUGH!" Angela yells, as blood seeps from her many wounds. Lola grins, her face a mask of many thoughts. She is enshroud with sand, her sweater and slacks now a dusty grey. She snaps out at Angela, mischief in her mind.

"It will never be enough! I want to *feed and fuck*" she protests as she rubs her body seductively.

For the first time in centuries, Angela wonders if she has made a mistake. She raises slowly, her dominion having encircled their intimacy with lust in their eyes.

All is quiet as the groups' heavy gaze rests upon her. Angela realizes that her fold has witnessed her in a vulnerable state, and this should not be so. Yet the 'new one' has taken her emotions by surprise and has caused her to show weakness.

"You will do as I say and come. The sun is near and we must reach the caves," she states as she tries desperately to regain control.

"Yes," Rinella interjects, "Again we will sleep in the dreaded caves because you have wasted time giving the gift to yet another who deserves it not."

Angela pauses, shock on her face. Could it be her most trusted has called her out? Made a mockery of her while the new one defies her? She is caught and momentarily finds herself at a loss for words.

Lola smiles seductively at Rinella. "Are you jealous? Mad because you didn't get any? It was so good too!"

Rinella moves swiftly and takes the hair of her new foe into her fingers! She uses all the strength she possesses to twist her to the ground.

Angela sees this and yet she cannot move! She watches as Rinella throws Lola to the sand and extends her fangs to sink them into her throat. As Lola struggles to become unpinned, and the waves of the ocean crash ever closer, the one who has led this group shakes her head to clear her thoughts.

"ENOUGH!" she screams, her eyes ablaze. She levitates and glides towards the women; the sternness in her voice regains control of this unexpected situation.

Rinella stops in mid-motion. Lola ceases her struggle, the look of defiance written all over her face.

"What has you riled, Rinella? What makes you defy me and go against my wishes?"

Rinella disengages herself and stands before Angela in the darkness. The need to eat and the other need, has fled. She glares at Angela, her fangs exposed.

"I do not like this one! She is trouble and I feel it!"

Lola stands, her hunger insatiable, and because she is newly made, she is unaware of the dangers of slaying one of her own kind. So she eyes both Angela and Rinella, weighing her options.

"Well now, you make a bold statement and undermine my authority," Angela states with false sugar dripping from her voice. "You do not like my choices and that disturbs me," she continues, as she runs a sharp nail along Rinella's throbbing artery.

"Let me eat this bitch!" Lola suddenly shrieks! "You'd better let us settle this now!"

"What do you know?" Rinella screams. "You, in the fold less than a sunrise and yet dare to make demands!"

Angela feels her hold slip on the situation yet again. Lola poses a huge problem, and she feels Rinella's' insecurities. The sun approaches and she has not settled the problem of nighttime habituations. The others of her fold stand by, uncertain, with hunger in their eyes.

"Stop this thing you do!" Angela says, her voice rising above the sound of the crashing waves.

Lola laughs, her body thirsting for the unknown. She has always been the underprivileged, underappreciated, underpaid, and under loved. She feels drawn to this woman, and yet she also feels defiant!

"She picked the wrong motherfucker to mess with!" she thinks, as she watches Rinella closely.

"Oh, the orgasm was really sweet, and I would love to stay and chat, but I got business to take care of!" she says to Angela.

The deep wrinkles in the lead Vampyres brow, shows her displeasure. "Do you defy me so soon little one?"

"Oh you have made a big mistake tonight! I don't answer to anyone sweetheart, and this you can count on," Lola hisses with newfound spirit."

Angela is appalled at Lola's defiance! She bares her fangs and prepares to end the fledglings' short, immortal life! Rinella grins as she recognizes Angela's intentions.

Lola also sees that this has turned bad and decides to leave. She levitates and flies up into the night sky a split second before the irate Vampyre can reach her.

CHAPTER THIRTEEN

Patricia Moore watches as the forensic scientist places the severed head into the evidence bag. The beach is deserted and she thanks God for small favors. The sun is unusually strong for this time of the year, and normally there would be people about.

"I believe we have ourselves a serial killer," her partner Detective Jackie Price states. She stifles a gag and removes her dark shades. "The club, this damn head, and not to mention countless missing persons; Pat this is some scary shit!"

"I know, just didn't want to admit it. Okay let forensics do their thing, my ass is going to have a drink," Patricia responds and makes her way back to the unmarked sedan.

"I second that emotion!" Jackie says as she trots behind her partner and friend.

Patricia removes her side arm and eases into the car. She is a petite woman, standing only five foot four inches. She sports short honey blonde hair which accentuates her light complexion.

Freckles cover her face and add to her 'cute' charm. Deep set brown eyes are filled with intelligence and her long angular nose suggests a mixed heritage.

"A double whiskey is what I'm thinking," Jackie says as she enters the car and slams the door. "This has been the weirdest fucking week of my career. You have any ideas?"

Patricia starts the car and backs out of the parking space. "I don't have a fucking clue, but we better figure this shit out quick! The media will jump all over the department if we don't come up with some answers."

They drive silently along PCH towards the little cabana that they frequent, often on duty. This is their 'beat' and everyone knows and respects the women for their fairness, if not total integrity.

Jackie looks out of the window, her thick brow knitted together with worry. She has grown up here in Long Beach, been a protector of it for the past ten years, and it worries her that someone is going up and down the beautiful, peaceful beach, tearing people's heads off.

"Man this shit is baffling!" she says as they near the bar. "The shit at the club for instance, now, who could have come into a bar full of people and do that much damage, without anyone at least wounding the fucker?" she asks her partner.

Patricia rolls the car into an empty space in front of 'Ricky's Cabana,' and parks. She turns off the ignition and rubs her temples. Deep in thought, she blocks out Jackie's words.

"Oh I know who can do just that!" she thinks, careful not to speak her words aloud.

Patricia is a cop by day but a hunter by night. She comes from a long line of Vampyre hunters and this is her deepest secret. Hell, the only reason she became a cop was for the convenient cover. Hunt and turn the demons to ash by night, and cover up her work by day.

"Sasha," she thinks, *"I have been chasing that bitch for years and have never seen her be this brazen!" What the fuck has made her do damage like this?"*

Aloud, Patricia says, "Let's get that drink, shit I can't even think right now,"

Jackie nods her head in agreement and the women exit the car, both looking forward to a much needed drink.

Donna hasn't eaten in two days. She has obsessively called her mother every hour on the hour.

"Chile I said everything is fine!" her mother states, for the third time today. "What's gotten into you, baby? I don't hear from you for weeks and now I can't get you to stop calling! Now tell me what's really on your mind."

Donna gnaws at her nails, her eyes on the window. The day has faded away and night draws near. Since the episode with Sasha she finds herself quite afraid of the dark. She also has questioned her faith and this disturbs her.

"Nothing is wrong Ma, just miss you is all."

"Well I have to go baby, my show is coming on and you better not call while I'm watching because you know I won't answer!"

Donna reluctantly says goodbye and gently hangs up the phone. Her heart is beating a mile a minute and her gnawing has drawn blood. She reaches for the Bible which lays on her nightstand, but can't seem to concentrate long enough to read.

"Lord, have mercy on me! I never would have believed in any shit like this, but I can still smell her in my closet!"

Suddenly, as quickly as night has come, there is a scratching at the window! She hugs the book to her bosom and stares out at the face that has suddenly appeared.

"Renee!" she exclaims, the fear mounting instead of fading away at the sight of her friend's familiar face.

Slowly she goes to the window, the Bible still against her breast. Renee levitates outside the window, a soft smile on her lips.

"Open the window," she whisper, and suddenly Donna is terrified! She hesitates, not sure if she about to make the biggest mistake of her life.

"You alone?" are the only words she can bring herself to utter.

"Of course I am and get that look off your face Donna! You know I would never hurt you!"

"I know you wouldn't but what about the other chick?" she asks, one hand now on her hip.

Renee laughs, careful to keep her fangs hidden. It is the sound of her friend laughing that causes Donna to unlock the window. The memories of all they have shared, all that Renee has given her. Her fears have receded, but the Bible she does not relinquish. She steps aside and allows her entry.

"The chick that saved you slept in your closet and left you alive? That chick?" she asks as she lands softly on the carpet.

Donna looks at her stealth form, dressed in green slacks and blouse, a long leather jacket brushing against black suede boots.

"You dress like her too! That bitch put the 'hoodoo' on your ass? What the fuck happened?" I would have died before I believed in Vampires and shit, but fuck I was wrong! Those motherfuckers are all over this damn city!" Donna says a little too loudly.

Renee removes the jacket and tosses it on the bed. She makes her way to the kitchen as Donna follows.

"It's quite a story Donna, and one that has no ending. Sasha fucked me then bit my ass, it's that simple," she states as she opens the refrigerator.

Donna watches in amazement as she takes a bottle of wine out and pours herself a large glass full. As she drinks, she realizes why Donna stares so intently.

Laughing, she explains, "Yes I can still eat and drink! Stop looking like that," she says as her eyes move down to the book in Donna's hand. "Please put that away, it hurts me to look at!" she says rather harshly.

Donna hesitates momentarily, but in the end she opens a nearby drawer and delicately places the Bible therein.

Relief floods Renee's face and she embraces Donna who tenses in fear. "Oh shit! Did I do the right thing?" she thinks, and by the look on Renee's face, she can tell that she has somehow read this thought.

"You offend me Donna; you should know that I mean you no harm. If not for me Sasha would have made mincemeat of you by now," she says as she steps away and finishes the wine.

"Speaking of which, where is the 'Queen' this evening? I can't imagine her letting you out without her. When she left here she said to forget about you. What's up with that?" Donna takes the wine and drinks from the bottle.

"Picked up on that jealousy thing did you? Well that's how she is and I guess I can live with that. She knows I am here. I told her that I needed you to do a few things for me. I need your help, so to speak. Some things I can't take care of at night."

"Oh fuck no! You want to make my ass a zombie or some shit?"

Just as Renee prepares to answer, a sound comes from the bedroom.

"What the hell was that?" Donna questions.

"You left the window open?" Renee whispers, and begins to sniff the air.

"Shit! There is a Vampyre in this fucking place and it isn't Sasha!"

"Well who the fuck is it?" Donna whispers back, as more sounds come from the bedroom.

"Donna, listen to me, get out of here quick!"

"You aint said nothing but a word!"

Just as she turns for the front door, Rinella blocks the path.

"Tsk Tsk! Now where do you think you are going?"

Renee pulls Donna to her by the collar of her shirt. She throws her back toward the counter and flies at Rinella who screams in fury!

"Come on you bitch!" she yells as Renee pushes her back into a wall. The force causes the apartment to rumble.

"You think you are any match for me? I am RI-NELLA!"

The Vampyres exchange fierce blows! Rinella catches Renee under the jaw with a left hook that sends her hurling into the living room. Quick as lightening Renee is up and digging her long nails into the others throat!

Donna watches as the women claw, bite, tear and wrestle through the apartment, tearing her shit up in the process!

She sees that Rinella is indeed stronger and has begun to get the better of a bloodied Renee. Thinking quickly she grabs the Bible from the drawer and eases her way into the hallway where the two are currently entangled.

Renee has her fangs exposed, blood drips from them and the sight causes a sadness to overwhelm Donna.

Rinella is atop Renee, reaching for her jugular with all her might, fangs straining to reach their mark.

"Hey!" Donna shouts and as the demon turns, she places the book upon her cheek.

The roar is deafening! The Vampyre is thrown back against the far wall, her face burning away on one side! She screams in agony and thrashes about the floor. Her face appears to literally melt away.

Renee gathers her battered body from the floor and stands. Her body begins to slowly heal itself but she staggers, obviously weak.

"Open up in there! This is the police!" Shouts and banging on the front door!

Renee turns, her eyes round with surprise.

"I have to get out of here Donna, I'm sorry but I have to go!"

Donna looks at the front door, unsure of what to do. Suddenly she pushes Renee down the hall and back into the bedroom.

"Go honey; get the fuck out of here! I'll handle this…"

Out of the hall flies Rinella, half of her face missing. She grabs Donna and flies past Renee, through the open window, with her prey, into the night.

CHAPTER FOURTEEN

Sasha has feed well tonight. She was furious when Renee insisted on visiting Donna, but had given in after another long and lazy session of lovemaking.

"That's okay, I will let it be for now, but trust me, I will eventually devour that bitch!"

Suddenly, Sasha's body tenses and she *sees* through Renee's eyes! One of Angela's folds is trying to kill her beloved! Sasha begins to will her way to Donna's apartment, when all of a sudden; a familiar voice speaks to her from the shadows.

"Sasha, Queen of all things unholy!"

Sasha turns to face Patricia the Hunter. It has been years since they were this close to one another, and Sasha is uneager to do this dance at the moment.

"Pat, I thought you were down South, but I should have known that you would follow me," Sasha states as she takes a step back.

"Now you know I won't rest until you are dust in the wind," she answers innocently.

The vision of Rinella fleeing through an open window with Donna flashes before Sasha's eyes and her pulse quickens. Renee is weak and calling to her for help!

"Your father and his father before him could not stop me Pat, so what makes you think you can? I have walked this earth from time before time and have dealt with the likes of you quite easily.

"I could end your life in the blink of an eye; however, I have grown quite fond of you, believe it or not! I have even thought of offering you the dark gift," Sasha continues as she takes another step backwards.

Pat averts her eyes from those of Sasha, and shakes her head as if to clear it. "I know your strength Sasha, and can tell that you are distracted. I didn't come here to kill you; instead I want to ask a question. Are you responsible for the recent murders in the city? They don't seem to be your style."

"Pat, I would love more than anything to stand here and watch you do the dance, try to kill me in other words. However, I have other matters to attend to just now. But to be fair, I will say that the overt massacres are not of my doing! You have been on my heels since I slew your beloved father, and you know I don't like attention."

Pat cringes at the reference to her father, and reaches into her pocket. Her hands are stilled as Sasha forces her will upon her. Deeper in the shadows, Sasha senses another, newly made Vampyre, and has to still her curiosity. Bemused, she reaches out to Renee and thinks, *"I am coming my darling! Do not go after Rinella alone!"*

"I don't have time for this Pat the Hunter! I have a feeling that we will meet again, and soon. For now, I will leave you with this: there is one that you also know, one that I made in a moment of weakness. Angela, remember her? Look to the caves and you will find her and the fledglings she has made out of contempt for me!"

Sasha is then gone upon the night breeze, leaving Pat to stare in amazement at the empty spot she has vacated. Her body loosens and she caresses the silver relic in her pocket.

She'd known that Sasha would be here, amid the lights of Downtown Long Beach. She'd also known this wouldn't be a good time to try for slaying; Sasha had to be taken down with a lot of thought. She'd had her cornered many a time, but that bitch is good!

Now she takes heed of Sasha's words and takes out her phone to Google the various caves in the area.

The newly reborn Lola watches the exchange between Sasha and the cop. She is hungry and has quietly been following the pretty police officer with the hopes of feasting upon her tender flesh.

Just as she began her attack, she sensed the sexual allure of Sasha and stopped, her mouth agape, as she lays her eyes upon the Queen for the first time.

Confusion takes hold of her thoughts as she moves back, deeper into the night. She salivates as her red eyes move between the cop and the one like unto her.

"She is beautiful!" Lola thinks her stomach in knots, from excitement as well as hunger. She weighs her options and wisely decides not to challenge this woman! She feels the strength of her as it emanates from her very pores! Ahh, but she will feast upon the cop! Of this she is certain!

"*If you touch her, I will end your short life fledgling!*" reverberates suddenly inside her head! Lola shrinks back, her fangs exposed.

Sasha vanishes, but her words linger on. *"The cop is off limits! Besides, she would kill you as sure as you stand! Leave this place and I will suffer you to live a little longer, Lola! Yes, I know you; I know all and do not doubt me!"*

Lola bares her teeth and reluctantly watches the cop take out her phone. Her body is in spasms from her hunger, yet she is inexplicitly drawn to Sasha. She sniffs the night air and leaps into the air to follow the Queen of Darkness.

Renee stumbles towards the window and screams, "Noooo! Donna!!" She leaps from the window, her nose following the scent of the burning scavenger. **"Donna, I am coming for you! Sasha! Help me baby!! Please come to me!"**

The lights of the harbor fly past, beneath her as she glides along the breeze. *"Do not go after them alone!"* Sasha screams, inside her head. *"I swear that bitch is more trouble than she is worth Renee!"*

"You have got to help her! She wounded Rinella and she will surely kill her! Sasha, if you love me..."

Rinella heads towards the caves as Donna struggles beneath her. She has the bitch in her strongest embrace, but is weak from the contact with the Holy Word.

"Be still you cunt!" she admonishes, as Donna scratches and claws at her hands. Rinella's face is a hot ball of fire and she can't wait to rip the throat from this one! Angela would be furious, however, if she does not deliver her the prey.

Minutes from her destination, she realizes that the wound is spreading instead of healing. "I should drop you to the ground below and watch your brains splatter just for the fun of it you meddling bitch! How dare you strike me?"

"Fuck you!" Donna screams between breaths. She twists her head to look at the ground far below. She is aware that she is dangerously close to passing out. The air is thin, and Donna is short of breath. *Please Lord, help me!"* she prays aloud.

Rinella screams in fury! "Shut the hell up!"

"I don't want to die Father!" Donna prays, as she gasps for air. Her protruding eyes begin to lose focus, the freezing wind causes tear to well in her eyes.

Donna draws from all the faith she can muster and allows her body to relax. She sees the ocean below and decides that death by drowning would be far better than the death this foul *'thing,'* has in store for her.

Suddenly, she is startled to hear Sasha inside her head: ***"It is I, Sasha, who will answer your prayer woman! Not you're invisible God! Be prepared to fall…"***

From the darkness comes Sasha's hand. She takes hold of Renee, her hair sailing behind her. Dark red eyes penetrate into the heart of Renee and she feels her crimson tears as they run down her face. Sasha has come! "Sasha, do something! I'm not as strong as you! Stop her!"

Sasha grins in spite of herself. The sight of her beloved causes her to do some crazy things! Oh, but she has not forgotten herself! This is a temporary state of mind. The cure for her loneliness has stolen her heart and mind, and with the coming of dawn she accepts that she will do anything and risk anything, for the woman before her.

She has tousled inside of Renee's mind and knows that a small piece of her resents Sasha for giving her the gift, but for now this is okay. She relishes in the very scent of Renee! To save this human, for now, is of no consequence.

She reaches out to Donna and recoils at the thoughts of her mind. The very existence of God is true, and Sasha has no desire to face him or one of his Angels, just now. As Donna relaxes her body and plots to reach for Rinella's weak spot, she stills the woman with her thoughts.

"Renee, my love, you will have to catch your beloved friend while I deal with Rinella and 'the other…'"

Renee turns and embraces Sasha, her tongue out for a caress. "Do it! But *what* other…"

Donna feels a gathering force as Sasha appears from nowhere, at her side. Rinella shrieks in surprise as her body is contorted and Donna is released from her grip! "No! You bitch!" Sasha pushes her through the air and she is flailing! Her wounds deepen as her strength fails.

Hate pours from her body in spurts.

"You again!" she shouts to Sasha. "Oh you are gonna die bitch!"

"I doubt by your hand! You are no match for me, and should've stayed with your Maker this night!" With that, Sasha moves with the speed of sound, her coat suddenly a twirl of blades! She stretches her hands as she flies towards the weakened Vampyre.

Rinella thinks of three things as Sasha approaches: one, her body was failing. She'd not yet eaten and the wound is rapidly devouring her body. Two, this bitch has blades in the underling of her coat, and they are currently headed straight for her. And three, Angela is the only one even close to dealing with Sasha's strength!

CHAPTER FIFTEEN

Lola watches, bewildered. The beautiful Vampyre of old is saving the human's life! And her lover! Exquisite! Lola feels confusion at her desires. She is drawn to them both. Yet her hunger has not been sated and her body begins to tremble.

Visions of her teeth as they sink into warm flesh and the feeling of hot blood squirting, hitting the back of her throat, invade her with a force so strong, that she momentarily loses interest and can think of nothing but to kill. She sniffs deeply in, the night air, and the smell of human blood nearby overwhelms her.

She changes direction on the wind, and uses her keen eyesight to hone in on the streets below. The city sleeps, but as usual there are those who can't resist the call of the night.

It is well past closing time for the various bars and clubs that crowd the newly renovated downtown area, yet there are couples strolling along and small groups of partygoers staggering off to the wherever next after party may be.

Lola spots a heavyset man as he enters an underground parking structure. She glides towards the structure and lands softly upon the pavement.

Donna drops from her captives arms, the earth rapidly approaching. She screams for dear life, calling out God's name. *"Please Lord!!"* Her heavy frame is weightless as she falls freely. She notes how lovely the lights are, just as she succumbs to defeat.

Renee waits for the moment when Sasha releases her and changes her direction. She is no longer flying forward, but down, towards the lights. The beating she sustained earlier has an effect as her body struggles to heal. She realizes then, that Sasha is indeed unique, and has earned the title of ALL.

She briefly remembers the moment she'd glimpsed Sasha as she had been before she was bitten. Sasha roaming through a village filled with carnage. Her young face a mask of confusion.

Donna's cries still these random thoughts and Renee gathers speed, propelling her suddenly tired body towards Donna's falling one.

Angela mopes, bewildered as to how she has lost control. The fresh taste of blood on her lips does nothing to calm her nerves.

"First that little asshole gets away from me, and now Rinella is late!" she screams, her naked body slithering to and fro. The cave stinks of rotting flesh, and the few minions left to her disposal are crouched along a wall in fear.

"Where is she? Wait…"

Angela walks to the mouth of the shallow cave and stands beneath the full moon. Her nostrils flare as she inhales the ocean air. Recognition dawns in her eyes and she growls, crimson sweat dripping into her seductive eyes.

"To me!" she yells as she rushes into the cave and in one motion, she is clad in leather pants and vest. Her darkest fear is about to be realized! Rinella is in the clutches of that self proclaimed 'Queen'!

"Stupid, BITCH! I will see her dead if it's the last thing I do!" She leads her minion out of the cave, and into the waning night.

They fly beside her, and she thinks, not for the first time tonight, that she should not have engaged Sasha. No matter what has transpired, she still understands that the years of Sasha are innumerable! She is really no match for her, yet in her conceit she thinks she can out smart her.

"Master, I see Rinella!" one of her companion yells as they approach a tangle of bodies suspended in mid-air. The group swoops to a stop at the heels of Sasha. She holds Rinella by the shoulders, her fangs embedded deep into her neck, several blades from the underlining of her coat, cutting into Rinella's limp body.

Blood, black as coal, runs down the twisted body, and Sasha turns to the newly arrived Angela, and spits the concoction into her face.

"No! Rinella, my darling!" shouts Angela. "Sasha, you are a cunt from the dark pits of HELL!"

Sasha laughs and drops Rinella's body. The group watches her fall, down, passing the forms of Renee and Donna.

"Angela, you are a disappointment to me! I thought I taught you; never send a fledgling to do a Vampyres job. I tire of you and your games. Tonight may be the night that your miserable life ends, for good this time!" she states as she draws her sword.

"Sasha!" Renee wails. She has caught Donna in mid air and is headed back inland, towards Sasha's closer, home. "The sun will rise soon! Stop fucking around and kill her ass!"

Angela hisses just as Sasha flies towards her, the sword aimed right at her heart! Black, one of her fledgling, suddenly swoops between her and the sword, and takes the hit. One moment her large frame is there, and the next she a skeleton, disintegrating into ash.

Sasha watches Blacks' large eyes open in shock, just before the silver tip of the sword buries itself, to the hilt, into her soft flesh. Then, like so many before her, she crumbles back into the dust from which her body was formed.

Angela rolls away from the next attack and calls to the remaining of her flock to retreat to the caves. She flies with all the speed she can muster, away from Sasha. The ocean lay below them, the caves just west of The Vincent St. Thomas Bridge. She must reach them. She cannot die here tonight!

Lola floats into the garage and allows her nose to lead her to the warm blood which flows through the unfortunate man. She hears his footsteps echo through the deserted structure and wills her mind into his thoughts.

"I can't get another DUI, got to sober up!"

She can suddenly smell the alcohol as it radiates from his pores.

She does not think anything of this, being newly made, she thinks only of the hunger pangs as they wrack through her body. She becomes simultaneously light headed and aroused as she draws within sight of him. He has taken out a key ring and examines each one to determine which one opens the door.

Lola lands softly behind him and watches as he struggles to focus on the keys. He turns slightly and catches her out of the corner of his eye. The man sways on his feet; he lowers his arms and squints at the woman before him.

"Well now, what can I do fer ya?" he asks, as Lola extends her arms and fangs, and lunges for him.

She reaches the startled man and yanks him to her awaiting teeth. The keys fall to the ground and instantly he claws at her wrist as she tears into his flesh.

The blood rushes down her throat and she gorges on her feast. The moment arrives when she feels her dead heart beat and his life force shoot through her veins! The feeling is better than that of any orgasm she has ever given herself! Her strength keeps the thrashing man in check, and to anyone happening to pass, they appear to be two lovers in a tight embrace.

She lifts him briefly from his feet and drains the last of him. His body goes limp in her arms and she tosses him against the wall in front of the car. Lola wipes her dripping fingers and licks her fingers. Then she feels unsteady on her feet.

The alcohol content of the blood hits her suddenly and she sees double!

"What the fuck?" she whispers. She turns to leave the place of her kill, struggling to control the unexpected effects of the blood. To her horror, she senses the suns arrival!

Lola resides across the waterway, in San Pedro. In her new excited state, and having endured the craziest evening of her life, she has neglected to stop and consider that she could die in daylight! She levitates and flies crookedly out of the garage.

To her advantage, she flies west, away from the rising sun. Her stomach dry heaves and a new pain seizes her body. The alcohol courses through her veins and she wonders how long the effect will last. So much that she doesn't know or understands!

"Damn! Should I have stayed with the one who made me a little while? What if I drink from someone who is sick? Will their infections pass on to me like the alcohol did?" she questions the empty air. She will have to consider these things later; right now she must get to her tiny apartment and find the darkest corner in which to hide her body!

Lola reaches her home and slips in through the open bedroom window. Esme, her black cat, watches her enter from the bed. The cat stands and arcs her back, as she hisses at Lola.

"It's me baby," Lola croons to the cat. She closes the window and shade, the room not nearly as dark as it needs to be. She shoos the cat off the bed and pulls off the blanket. Levitating, she drapes the blanket over the window as she notes the difference it makes to the room.

Esme looks up at her floating form and scurries from the room. The cat runs to the living room and hides under the couch.

Lola strips out of her clothing and grabs her throbbing temples. She was not a drinker in her human life, and now she remembers why. That fucking hangover feeling! She stumbles around the room and thinks of the best place to sleep.

Her mind wonders back to all the old Vampire movies she has seen, and the vision of a coffin invades her cloudy mind.

"I guess we really do sleep in coffins," she thinks, the picture inviting. At the moment she does not possess one so best leave that thought alone, as the sudden fear of burning to death takes hold of her.

She flings open the bedroom closet door and curses when the small space is revealed. "Shit!" she yells, the space behind the window becoming brighter. She has no choice but to toss out the closets contents, pull a thick blanket down from its shelf, close the door securely, and bury her body within.

CHAPTER SIXTEEN

Pat drives along Western Avenue, towards San Pedro. She knows of the cliffs at the end of land to the south. There have been many fatal accidents along the shore on that particular stretch of the sea. Many missing hikers have been found, dead, at the base of the sheer Montesano Cliffs.

That would be an ideal place for a group of Vampire to hide out. She'd had little reason to venture here, the weird slayings having only recently begun.

She'd decided to search the caves in the daylight and use the surprise attack to her advantage. The caves were really just one giant coffin and so she had no doubt that the coven were there.

A group of startled Vampire would be easy pickings with nowhere to run. Pat had the slaying of over one hundred of the beast under her belt, and felt confident that this would be a piece of cake.

She fingered the ancient medallion of silver in her hand, and let her mind settle on thoughts of Sasha.

For years she'd hunted Sasha in New Orleans, the city of her birth. Through the city, through the swamps, above ground and below, she'd followed.

Hell bent on destroying that which had so soundly defeated her beloved father, she risked limb and life to kill her! But Sasha was always one step ahead of the hunter! Oh, she'd been close a few times, but Sasha had centuries of experience from which to draw.

During one of the times she'd had her close enough to slay, Sasha had mind fucked her out of reality, and nearly taken her life.

"Patricia," Sasha had spoken, her sensuous body covered by a flimsy layer of rose red perspiration, "let me make you my lover and give you pleasures beyond your comprehension!"

Patricia, sitting beneath the covers of her bed, half asleep and praying that she is dreaming, remembers staring at the beautiful figure and actually feeling her clitoris jump! The window was wide open, the curtains billowing out into the breeze.

"You were not invited to enter here Sasha!" she protested weakly. The sound of Sasha's laughter sent goose bumps down her spine.

Was she really attracted to this undead being? The one who'd ended the life of her father, her friend? Pat watched as Sasha allowed her coat to fall to the floor. She saw the buttons of her shirt undo themselves as Sasha's full breasts were slowly revealed.

Her smooth skin glistened as she stepped out of her tight jeans. In a flash, she stood before Pat wearing only a red laced pair of panties. Her nipples hardened against her will as she struggled to look away from Sasha hypnotic glare.

"Yet you have invited me darling, in your heart. I feel its irregular beat from here," Sasha declares, as she inches closer to the woman on the bed.

Then, she is there, next to Pat who is immobilized.

"Do you really wish to kill me?"

Pat is torn between a strange lust, and her need to destroy Sasha. She is still as Sasha moves the covers aside and runs a cold finger down her cleavage.

She is repulsed and turned on at the same time as Sasha leans forward and traces her tongue along the edges of her lips. Her fingers move lower and find their way between her legs.

Pat has a moment to regret years of sleeping in the nude, before she feels Sasha's long fingers caress her mound. She gasps and is appalled to find herself wanting to stick out her own tongue and meet Sasha's!

A wave of intense desire sweeps over her and she moves her hips against Sasha's rubbing fingers, her clit eager to release months of pent up pressure. She relaxes her body and is surprised that she is very near to exploding!

Then Sasha places her mouth against the side her neck. She feels the tips of her teeth, sharp and pointy, as they rest gently against her skin. "Shall we become one? The smell of your juices is intoxicating..."

Pat reaches her climax at the sound of Sasha's voice. Her body spasms and the urges to pull Sasha atop of her body are strong. Yet as she opens her eyes, she sees the picture of her handsome father on the nearby dresser.

Pat turns on a switch inside of her head, and quickly becomes the cold hearted detective that she is known as around the city.

She reaches quickly to her left in search of the special medallion that has been passed down to her for such an occasion as this. She is not quick enough, however, and hears Sasha hiss and feels her presence recede in the darkness.

Pat reaches and turns on the bed lamp beside her and is stunned to see that she is alone. There is no trace of Sasha; the only evidence of their encounter is the sticky wetness between her legs.

The car runs smoothly as Pat pulls herself from the past. She is disgusted with herself, as usual, at the thought of having allowed a Vampire to seduce her, but thankful that she herself hadn't become one of the undead.

She realizes that Sasha could've easily bitten her that fateful night, and often wonders why the Queen had elected to spare her. Part of her believed that it was part of some twisted game that Sasha enjoyed playing with her: the hunted turning the tables on the hunter.

"Why didn't you try to kill her last night?" she wondered aloud, just as her cell phone sprang to life and greeted her with the sounds of Tamia's 'So into you.'

"This is Pat," she answers.

"Pat, looks like we got another one," her partners voice replies.

Pat shakes her head and looks through her rearview mirror.

"What we got?"

"Male victim in the 2nd Street parking garage, level one. Pat, his throat has been ripped out and there's not a drop of blood anywhere! Where are you? I think you need to get over here pronto."

"How long has he been dead?" she asks.

Jackie looks at the scene and chokes back her breakfast. "Not sure, forensics hasn't arrived but the poor guy doesn't look as if he has been here long," she responds as she turns and heads for the squad car.

Pat makes a u-turn and curses under her breath. "I'm on my way. Be there in about fifteen minutes. Jackie?"

"Yeah Pat?"

"Don't let LBPD touch anything, you hear me? There may be something that will help us catch the perp!"

"Ten-four, Pat, I got it, just get your ass down here! I'm starting to get the willies for real!"

Pat hangs up the phone and leans her head back against the seat. She regrets having to wait to try to catch Angela and the other Vampire who are eating their way through the city. Things had been quiet for awhile but now the shit was hitting the fan!

"Fuck me! How many of them are there? How many has Angela made?" she wondered.

She'd wanted to make an excuse and have Jackie take this one alone, but she knew there would be too many questions if she didn't join her partner. If Jackie even suspected what was going on, and more, that Pat is involved to a degree, the young woman would probably lose her mind.

So she headed back to Long Beach, hoping that she would have enough time before sunset tonight, to search the caves before the clan has a chance to relocate.

CHAPTER SEVENTEEN

Donna sat and stared at the two coffins, her mind on the verge of a nervous breakdown. She relived the moments, yet again, of Sasha's sword and blades flying through the air and making dust of everything they encountered.

Renee had flown her away from the carnage, but not before her eyes had witnessed the tirade. The younger Vampires had willingly positioned themselves between Angela and Sasha, almost as if in a trance, and Sasha found each of them and sent them to their deaths.

The last sight Donna had seen was that of Angela fleeing away from the peeking sun, and Sasha watching her go.

"Sasha!" Renee called, as she'd held Donna like a baby, in the crook of her arms. "The sun is coming up! Forget about her now, let's go baby!" At the sound of her voice, Sasha turned and flew to join them.

She gazed sternly at Donna then put her hand on Renee's waist. "She is bruised but not badly, so I expect to see Angela again. I doubt she goes away quietly!

She will try harder than ever to get to your friend, mostly because her pride is hurt."

"Why did you toy with her?" Renee asked fury in her voice. "You could've easily sent her to her death but you didn't, why?"

Sasha does not answer; instead she flies ahead and enters the window to her apartment with Renee and Donna at her heels.

Renee directs Donna to sit on a nearby sofa as she studies Sasha.

"What's going on with you and Angela? Didn't you say you tried to kill her before? What happened?"

Sasha strips out of her clothing much to the surprise of Donna, who sits clutching the sofa. She has her feet planted firmly on the floor, and wishes never to be off the ground again! She thanks God over and over again in her mind, for getting her safely away from Rinella.

"This is no time to talk Renee; we have only a few minutes before we slumber," she states as she strolls over to Donna and stands before her.

"You have been through this before, *human,* so you know the drill. You will not disturb our sleep, nor will you leave this place!"

Renee moves between Sasha and Donna, her body beginning to weaken from lack of feeding. Sasha looks into her eyes, and then kisses her lips.

"You need to feed my darling! You must learn that to feed is priority number one! Not running all over creation chasing after humans that you don't intend to feast upon!" Sasha admonishes.

She caresses Renee, her eyes resting on Donna. "Or do you wish to come to your senses and eat what is available to you?" Sasha asks coyly.

Donna is appalled to see her best friend lick her lips and shiver. She looks around the dimly lit room for an exit! Just as she decides to take her chances and run from the room, Renee sits beside her and exhales slowly.

"Donna, I would never do a thing like that to you!" Renee says soothingly, but Donna doesn't exactly trust her friend just now. Renee's breathing is labored and she has moved closer still to Donna.

"Umm, I don't want to be here Renee! Your eyes look funny to me!" Donna whispers.

Sasha watches the exchange with amusement in her eyes, and then suddenly she is gone from the room.

Donna begins to inch away from her hungry friend and those bright red eyes that stare at her. "After all we been through, you gonna just eat a sistah?" she asks.

Renee's body undergoes a change as the pounding of Donna's heart echo in her mind. She knows she could *never*... yet she is famished and can't think straight! She reaches out and grabs Donna by the arm, her fangs sliding out of their gums seemingly on their own.

The smell of fresh blood is strong in the air and Renee closes her eyes to regain control of her hunger.

"Renee, please!" Donna moans as she realizes there is no escape for her, if Renee decides she looks finger licking good! Her arm begins to hurt as Renee continues to tighten her hold.

Sasha watches from the doorway, a decanter of warm blood in her hand. She waits to see if Renee will give in to her nature and take the human who has caused so much trouble! It is interesting to see the new Vampyre struggle with the desires, and amusing to see the human plead for her life. In the end, however, Renee releases her friend and bows her head in shame.

"My love, drink this," Sasha directs as she gives the decanter to Renee.

"What?"

"Drink quickly! The sun has arisen and we must sleep," Sasha answers. "I always keep fresh blood and this is just one of the many things you have to learn in order to survive!"

Donna feels relief wash over her as Renee releases her. She sees Sasha hand her the drink and realizes she is looking at blood and not wine! Her stomach turns as she watches Renee drink greedily.

She drinks every drop of blood and Donna watches as her eyes go from deep red back to their natural color. She is nauseated and wants to wake up from this nightmare! She looks from Renee back to the naked form of Sasha and makes a vow to never look at another woman again if she gets out of this mess!

"Donna I wouldn't have hurt you, please believe that!" Renee states, her head hanging low. "Please stay here and we will talk about this tonight."

"You will stay here if you are smart," Sasha advises, as she takes Renee's hand. "The police are all over your apartment and will be looking for you soon."

"Oh shit!" Donna whispers as the two Vampyre head to another room. "What am I going to do?"

"Donna, try to get some sleep," Renee says to her frightened friend.

Sasha and Renee retired to their coffins, leaving Donna to sit and wait for nightfall. She is angry but doesn't dare leave and go home! Instead she feels sleep calling to her and giving in, sleeps like the dead.

CHAPTER EIGHTEEN

Angela limps into the rancid cave, her eyes balls of flames. She moves into the shadows and sits heavily down, her back against the far wall. Crimson tears spill down the wrinkles of her face, she having reverted back to her natural state.

Her dull hair hangs in clumps, her old and decrepit hands in her lap. She howls at the empty space before her curses the rising sun. All that she has lost over the past few days gnaw at her mind. Yuri, Dahlia and now Rinella! They had been at her side since she parted from Sasha so many years before and now she finds herself alone yet again.

She thinks of Lola and how she escaped her and this sends her into a new fury! She allows her battered body to heal itself while she calls out to everything unholy to curse Sasha and that bitch she has taken into her fold! "You will pay dearly for this Sasha! I will give you this battle but I, Angela, shall win the war!

A fat furry rat scurries out of a hole in the wall and Angela reaches out quickly and snatches the creature. She brings it to her lips and punctures its body with her sharp fangs. She sucks the struggling rats' blood dry and then flings the dead body into a corner.

Angela's body rejuvenates quicker with the small amount of blood she has ingested. She stands and is once again a beautiful woman full of youth and vigor. She is careful to stay away from mouth of the cave and the morning sunrays.

Briefly, she envisions her chambers beneath 'Claudia's' and again curses Sasha for her many loses. Then she retreats to the back of the cave and settles down to sleep. Before doing so, she reaches out for her newest fledglings mind and is amused to see her slumbering inside a small closet.

"You I will deal with first, my little traitor, and show you the consequence of defying me! First I will have my pleasure and then watch you die a horrible death!" she says, and grins into the darkness.

Patricia arrives at the crime scene and seeks out Jackie. She finds the detective near the rear of the victims' car.

"I see the coroner has pulled in," she says to Jackie.

"Yes, forensics has been here a few minutes but I don't think they will find anything," she answers as the two walks towards the body.

"The head is intact but otherwise it's the same as the bodies on the beach, and the ones at the club. This has got to be the work of the same person. Also, I just got a call for us to report back to the precinct."

Pat turns to her partner and frowns, "What's going on?"

"Well, there is a woman who says she has information about the murders at the club waiting in interrogation. There's not much to see here anyway, no witnesses, no fingerprints, no nothing. I told Garrison to send the report to us as soon as they get it logged."

"Damn! There's going to be a public panic once this gets out! Let's go talk to this woman and hope she has real information and not just after the reward."

Jackie nods her head as she watches the coroner pull out a heavy black body bag. "I don't know what's going on but I can tell you, I don't like it. Something strange is going on and I intend to find out what it is!"

The detectives leave the scene and drive the short distance to headquarters. Pat breathes deeply and tries to calm herself. She hadn't been through anything like this since coming to Long Beach, and hopes she can get control of the situation quickly.

"If I can find Angela and her coven then this will be over soon. I know Sasha and she will go deeper underground now that she knows I am here," she thinks.

Her thoughts are running all over the place and it is not until she and Jackie enter the interrogation room that she is fully in control of her emotions.

Gina doesn't want to talk to the police but Tyrone keeps throwing the reward money up in her face.

"We can use that money G! All you have to do is go down there and tell them what you saw! I know that bitch you were with must have seen something too," he shouts.

Gina regrets having mentioned that she and Donna were at the club the night of the murders. In her excitement at seeing the news report, she'd blurted out the tidbit while talking on the phone to her babies' daddy.

At first he'd pretended to be worried about whom she was out with and was she screwing that person.

"Who the hell is this 'friend' of yours and who was home watching my kids?" he questioned.

Gina rolled her eyes and explained that Donna was just an old high school friend. "We just went out for a quick drink Ty! I am always stuck here in the house and you don't bother coming over to check on me or your kids!"

Tyrone smacked his lips and continued, "So you fucking her uh? I know how you get down G. Don't forget it was my ass that turned you out. Remember Kim? Yeah, I know you remember her ass…"

The news is now focusing on the weather and so Gina turns off the television. She leans back against the couch and closes her eyes. She goes back to the night that she and Tyrone invited Kim to join them in their bed.

It was her first time having a threesome and although she'd done it to please him, she quickly found herself lost in ecstasy! The scent and taste of another woman took her to heights she had never dreamed possible! Her level of arousal was so intense, that several times she thought she would pass out.

"Yes, I remember Kim," she said dreamily.

"Well get out of lala land and tell me what happened at the club. That shit has been all over the news and they are offering a reward."

There really wasn't much to tell, yet Gina exaggerated a bit, hoping to keep Ty on the phone a little while longer. He called so rarely and she really did love him!

"So we hear this big commotion and we could *smell* the blood coming out of there! Then people started running out and I think the killer was this big dude wearing a Chargers' jersey but I can't be sure because by that time I got the hell out of there!" she lied.

"So this Donna chick actually went inside the joint?" Tyrone asked excitedly. "But you saw the dude right? Could you describe him to the cops?"

Gina thought about this particular lie and wondered if the police would buy a man coming out of a lesbian club. She didn't mention that fact to Ty, not wanting to expose the fact that she frequented that type of bar.

"Well, I was scared and there was so much going on Ty! I just remember that he was huge!"

"Call her and get her to tell you what she saw G. If she doesn't want some of that money, then that just means more for us!"

Of course Donna denied having seen anything when Gina called. She even sounded frightened, and Gina had never known Donna to be afraid of anything!

"Let it go and don't tell anyone you went there. Take my advice or some shit may visit you in the night!" those had been Donnas' exact words!

"Now why would she say some shit like that?" Gina wonders as she prepares to leave for the police station.

Tyrone lay in her bed, his smooth chest exposed to her from beneath the sheets. He'd come over last night to 'convince' her to go to the cops, and that meant he'd given her a courtesy screw. Gina accepted what he was willing to give, and woke this thoroughly satisfied, and willing to try to score the ten thousand dollar reward.

Detective Price was smarter than most people gave her credit for. She had been living in the shadow of her partner for more than a year now, and was perfectly content letting Pat take the glory for their various successes. She enjoys being a silent force, and staying 'low key.'

She has great intuition, a quality that can make any average detective into a great detective. Her intuition kicks in now as they question the supposed 'witness,' Gina

Sommers, a single mother of three who'd voluntarily come in claiming to have seen the man responsible for the carnage at 'Dahlia's.'

Jackie takes notes as Gina tells her story. She knows the woman is lying, and is sure it is the reward money she's after.

"So you saw a man, covered in blood come out of the club, right?" she asks the fidgety woman.

"Yes and he was a big dude too! He had blood all over his clothes."

"He came out of the club and ran right past you?" Pat interjects.

Donna begins to look nervous, and regrets having come here. She is beginning to forget her own story!

"No, I saw him from around the corner, I mean, he…"

Jackie stands abruptly and scowls at Gina.

"Look Miss Sommers, we could bust you for obstruction of justice just for coming in here and wasting our time! You should be ashamed of yourself! You think you are going to just be handed ten grand without us checking out your story?" she asks the frightened woman.

Pat glares at Gina as well. "Take a hike Miss Sommers."

"No! Listen, I was there! Just ask my friend Donna, she was there with me! I swear!"

Jackie turns and looks at Pat. Their eyes meet and Pat nods towards the door.

"We'll be right back," Jackie says to Gina.

The detectives leave the room and convene in the hall. Pat opens the file she has been holding.

"Donna James, you think that's who she's referring to?" she asks Jackie.

"If she is then that connects the club to the weird call Shan answered last night," she answers. "I tell you Pat, she was scared shitless when she came home last night!"

"Tell me again what she said, and don't leave anything out," Pat instructed, her eyes watching Jackie intensely.

"They answered a call last night, you know, loud screams, shit hitting the walls, so they thinking domestic violence. Anyway, Shan says that they could hear people fighting inside, then all of a sudden there's this unearthly scream!"

Pat stops her there, "Wait, what do you mean, 'unearthly?'"

Jackie shrugs her shoulders and shakes her head. "She couldn't explain it, just said it was like something out of a horror movie. All I know is that I had to stay awake and hold her all through the night.

She tossed and turned and woke up screaming a few times," she continues, sweat popping out on her brow.

"Jackie, why would she have nightmares about something she heard?" Pat questions.

"It wasn't what they heard, Pat. When they made entry the entire apartment was empty."

"*Empty?*"

"Yes, but the bedroom window was open and Shan says, well she *swears* that when she ran to the window, she saw…" Jackie whispers.

"What? What did she see Jackie?"

Jackie glances up and down the hallway to be sure no one can hear them. She grabs Pat and pulls her closer.

"She says she saw a woman fly off into the night."

CHAPTER NINETEEN

Evening draws near as Pat and Jackie sit outside Donna's Fourth floor apartment. They'd investigated the woman's home and Jackie discovered an ashy substance which she'd scraped into a small evidence bag, and was now currently studying.

She'd also spotted the Bible as it lay on the floor, the cover singed and covered in ash. She'd carefully placed it in a bag as well, and for the rest of their time inside, had held on to the tiny gold cross she wore around her neck.

"I have never seen anything like this Pat. It's like something burned, but what? And the smell! What the fuck was that odor?"

Pat continues to stare out of the window deep in thought.

"Fuck!" She thinks, *"This is turning bad. Of all the shit to find! If Jackie takes the evidence in to forensics then*

a whole new can of worms will open up. What the hell am I gonna do?"

Jackie looks from the evidence bag to her partner. She senses that Pat is withholding something from her but she holds her peace, with the hopes that Pat will eventually let her in on what she's thinking.

"So I guess Miss Sommers was telling the truth about being at the club, but I don't know about that male perp information she provided," Jackie says.

Pat turns to face her partner. She has grown fond of Jackie and has spent more than a few nights at she and her wife Shan's home drinking beer and playing cards. They are nice people and Jackie is a great detective but Pat knows that they wouldn't be able to deal with the fact that Vampyres existed.

Not only existed, but lived in nearly every city in America! Few people knew that they were not just something made up, but were real and have been for centuries.

"It's possible, although her story was a little mixed up. I just don't see how one man could've caused all that destruction," Pat says, as she rubs her temples, a serious headache having already begun.

"What about this uh," Jackie begins, as she takes a small notebook from her jacket pocket. "'Renee Larue?' Do you think that's someone we should look into?

When Pat and Angela returned to the interrogation room, they'd found Gina gnawing fretfully at her nails.

Pat got straight down to business. "Can you tell me your friend Donna's last name?"

Gina sat up straight, eager to tell them anything they wanted to hear, so that she could get the hell out of here, go home and smoke a blunt! She had begun to believe that they were going to lock her ass up!

"James, Donna James! She lives in Carson, I know the address too!"

Pat jots down notes, ready to be finished with Gina. She doesn't like the woman and is eager to make it to the caves before the Vampyre could rise tonight.

Jackie stood near the door, her thoughts moving between this strange case, and Shan, her police officer wife.

"Okay, we'll check out your story and call you if we need you to come back down," Pat said to Gina, and stood to escort her out.

Gina looked perplexed. "Umm, when do I get the reward money?"

Jackie stepped forward, her frame taller than that of Gina, and looked down at the bewildered woman.

"The reward is given upon the capture and *conviction* of the perpetrator or perpetrators! We haven't established that anything you have told us is true. Like my partner said," she concluded, as she'd taken Gina by the arm and directed her to the door, "we will call you if we need you further."

Gina's disappointment resonated on her face. *"Damn! Tyrone's gonnna be pissed!" she thought.*

"Okay and when you find her, ask her why she said I should be careful before something comes in the night and get my ass!"

Pat looked up, startled by these words but careful not to let it show.

Jackie, however, stopped the woman and asked her what she'd meant by that.

"Hell I don't know, but Donna knows something and I want it written down somewhere that I'm the one who told you! And if you can't find her at home, then she'll be at her friend Renee's house!"

"Renee? Who is she?" asked Jackie.

"She's Donna's best friend and when she's not at home or kicking it with me; she's at Renee's big penthouse in downtown L.A. Renee La something, some Cajun name. Larue! That's it, Renee Larue!"

"So you think she's worth looking into?" Jackie asks again when she fails to answer.

"That will be easy to do," Pat answers as she starts the car.

"Why do you say that?"

"Because she is a famous author, I have some of her books."

Shock shows on Jackie's face. "What?"

"Yep, she writes some of the scariest horror stories you'll ever read! Gruesome shit too!"

"Wait, so you're telling me that the murders at the club, the weird shit that happened here," Jackie says as she gestures towards the apartment building, "and a famous horror writer, are all connected?"

Pat nods her head and thinks, *"And I'll bet money that mixed up in all of this, is a centuries years old Vampyre who proclaims herself Queen!"*

A grin begins to spread across Jackie's face. She holds both evidence bags up before her.

"Let's get this to forensics and then go visit the writer. Maybe she's been writing creepy shit so long that now she's starting to *live* it!" she says enthusiastically. "I know she's involved!

Pat eases the sedan into traffic, her mind racing a thousand miles a minute. She can't allow the evidence to make it to forensics and she can't tell Jackie about the Vampyre.

She'd likely think Pat was a nut case and have her committed! Caught between a rock and a hard place, she weighs her options as the sun edges it's way West.

In New Orleans, she'd had a partner who stumbled upon her secret, and she'd killed her. She made it look as if the killer they were hunting was responsible, but in reality she'd shot her point blank, without even blinking. She was that serious about her secret life as a hunter.

Now it looks as if it will be necessary again.

"You're awfully quite over there. Are you okay?" Jackie asks, as she they roll down Torrance Boulevard.

"Yes, just thinking that we should follow up on an anonymous tip I received."

Jackie turns in her seat and thinks, *"so here we go keeping secrets. What's up with that? She knew Pat had been holding back!"* Aloud she said, "What tip? You didn't mention a tip."

Pat looks steadily ahead, forming the correct words in her mind before speaking.

"I got a call and all the caller said was, 'check the caves in San Pedro.' I didn't think anything of it, you know, thought it was some kid prank calling the station. But now, I don't think we should pass on even the tiniest lead. Like you said earlier, this is a strange ass case!"

"What would the caves have to do with this? Wait, you think someone is hiding in the caves? That what you thinking?" Jackie asks, as doubt clouds her face.

"You never know, and in one of Renee LaRue's books, the killer uses a cave to hide and dismember his victims," she lies.

At the mention of the author and the cave, Jackie perks up, just as Pat had known she would.

"Let her believe that bullshit if she wants to! I'll kill two birds with one stone: kill the coven of Vampyre and make it look like one of them kills Jackie!"

"You must be shitting me! Oh my God! This is like some shit straight out of a Hollywood movie.

So this writer, who writes horror novels, goes crazy and starts living out her books! She becomes a homicidal maniac and goes on a killing spree! Damn!" Jackie says through clenched teeth.

"Wouldn't that be something? And to be the detectives who solve the murders and make this city safe again! I pray it turns out to be that simple! This Renee woman might turn out to be responsible, in some way, for all the unsolved murders in this area for the past few months."

Jackie is animated, the two plastic bags and their contents, lay forgotten on the seat. Her mind is racing as she tries to put the pieces of the puzzle together.

"I still can't figure out what Shan saw out of that window though. That has me stumped. I mean, how did Donna James and whoever she was fighting with, get out of that apartment?"

"Yeah that is the one thing that's puzzling and I'll be sure to ask her when we see her ass," Pat answers.

"This has got to be the craziest case I have ever worked on! So we heading to check out those caves?" she questions as she checks her sidearm.

Pat chuckles inside and thinks how easy it is to steer her partner into her way of thinking. Her laughter is short lived; however, as she faces the fact that she is luring Jackie to her death.

She will take her life and cause pain to so many! And yet she sees no other way. The existence of Sasha and those like her must remain folklore. They must be thought of only as a person reads a book, watches a movie, or gazes upon a piece of art.

And she must continue her work, of ridding the world of Vampyre, one by one, while the world thinks it safely slumbers. Nothing must get in the way of her destiny, and she will die before dishonoring her heritage.

The sun begins to set on the city as they drive towards the harbor, as they drive towards redemption, as they drive towards death.

Made in the USA
Charleston, SC
31 October 2011